Guilty Pleasures

Books by Donald Barthelme

COME BACK, DR. CALIGARI
SNOW WHITE
UNSPEAKABLE PRACTICES, UNNATURAL ACTS
CITY LIFE
SADNESS

(For children)
THE SLIGHTLY IRREGULAR FIRE ENGINE

(Non-fiction)
GUILTY PLEASURES

Guilty Pleasures

DONALD BARTHELME

Farrar, Straus and Giroux · New York

"And Now Let's Hear It for the Ed Sullivan Show!" appeared
originally in Esquire *and "Games Are the Enemies of Beauty, Truth,
and Sleep, Amanda Said," in* Mademoiselle. *Except for these two and
for "The Teachings of Don B.," "Swallowing," "The Royal Treatment,"
"Bunny Image, Loss of: The Case of Bitsy S.," "The Expedition," "The
Angry Young Man," and "Mr. Foolfarm's Journal," all the pieces in
this book appeared originally in* The New Yorker.

The author wishes to thank The New York Times, Audience,
Fiction, *and* The Village Voice *for permission to reprint the pieces
which originally appeared in these publications.*

Library of Congress Cataloging in Publication Data
Barthelme, Donald.
    Guilty pleasures.
    I. Title.
PZ4.B285Gu [PS3552.A76]   813'.5'4   74-13193

To Joan, Pete, Rick, and Steve

The pieces in this book were written on all sorts of occasions and in response to all sorts of stimuli and overstimuli. The first third, roughly, are parodies. One always apologizes for writing parodies; it is a disreputable activity, ranking only a little higher on the scale of literary activity than plagiarism. A minimum demand is that what is parodied be widely successful—a tulip craze of some sort. This gives the parodist the luxury of being able to feel that he is doing useful work. A number of the pieces are political satire directed against a particular Administration. One can attempt to explain this Administration in a variety of ways, but *folie à deux* is perhaps too optimistic, and on the other hand I do not want to believe that we get what we deserve. Thus these efforts must be classified, I suppose, as simple expressions of stunned wonder at the fullness and mysteriousness of our political life.

The other pieces have to do with having one's coat pulled, frequently by five people in six directions. Some are brokeback fables and some are bastard reportage and some are pretexts for the pleasure of cutting up and pasting together pictures, a secret vice gone public. Guilty pleasures are the best.

D.B.

Contents

THREE

One

Down the Line with the Annual

The *Consumer Bulletin* is much used in courses in consumer problems, consumer education, economics, home economics, business, civics, marketing, sociology, life science, physics, and other business and science education subjects. Its findings provide valuable material to be used in teaching young consumers in high school and college how to become intelligent and informed buyers of goods and services, and to learn to look for sound qualities in the products they buy.

—Consumer Bulletin Annual

Will Candace come away with me—find integrity, wholeness on the Australian archipelago? Too early to say. Meanwhile, the affair of the Swedish tennis balls continues to plague us. I ventured into the basement, found Candace there on her knees before the washing machine, which was filled with Swedish tennis balls. Candace in tears. I took her hand. "What?" I said. "Oh, Charles," she said, "is everything galley-west? Everything?" I gave it some thought. Then: "You've been reading the *Annual*." She looked away. "It said these Swedish tennis balls could be washed in an automatic washer and dried in an automatic drier without deleterious effects. I had to *try*, didn't

3

I?" Washing machine has ineffective lint filter, which I
discovered last week when it strangled on new rug, 50
percent Dacron and 50 percent iron pyrites, purchased
by Candace without first looking it up in the imposing,
authoritative, annual *Annual*. Candace, however, is
blameless, racked as she is by irritation of the lungs from
overuse of aerosol hair sprays (page 15), unpleasant dry-
ing and crusting of the lips from overuse of indelible lip-
sticks (page 17). "I do not blame you, Candace," I said. "I
blame your inadequate education at that expensive Eastern girls' school." Iron-pyrites particles pulsing in her
golden hair. "Everything is galley-west," she whispered.
"Had I not yoyoed away my time in school reading
Herodotus, Saint-Simon, Rilke, and Owen Wister, seeking answers to the mystery of personality and the riddle
of history, I would not have failed to become an intelligent and informed buyer of goods and services. It's as
simple as that." And in her eyes there was a misty light,
produced by defective contact lenses (page 50).

Whirled my darling away to an ice-cream parlor, where
we consumed quantities of elephant's-foot ice (crammed
though it was with pernicious food additives). But the
problem remains. We are adrift in a tense and joyless
world that is falling apart at an accelerated rate. No way
to arrest the disintegration that menaces from every side.
Consider the case of the bedside clock. "Check for
loudness of tick," the *Annual* said. I checked. It ticked.
Tick seemed decorous. Once installed in home, it
boomed like a B-58. Candace watching it nervously,
neighbors complaining, calls from the police. And on
page 143 the electric can opener that sows tiny bits of
metal inside can being opened; on page 178 the sewing

machine whose upper thread tension is not indexed, whose cams do not produce the pictured patterns. Yes, they are mine. "There is no reason to believe that the eyes are permanently harmed by watching TV," the *Annual* says. (But what of insult to the brain?) "A good toaster should give successive slices of uniformly browned toast for many years." But my toaster brought to our union nothing but a significant shock hazard. And it is true that I purchased the nylon sheets that slide off the bed (page 211), the low-quality ink that dries too slowly (page 57)—my letters bleed through their envelopes like the hands of a medieval saint.

"It is estimated that some 5 million girls exist mainly on snacks of soft drinks, 'French fries,' pizzas, candy, hamburgers, and waffles." Who are these girls? What are their names? What do they look like? How does one get in touch with them? And how do they behave, fueled as they are with "foods of attractive appearance but dubious quality"? Candace wishes to send them lean beef in a plain brown wrapper. The freezer is full of it. (But then, the freezer itself is not trustworthy; it is given to broiling the meat in fits of temperature.) Let me confess it, I am tense, for this America is not the one I knew. I am going away, to the Australian archipelago, for although my pipe tobacco is of the type judged lowest in lead and arsenic in 1968 by the Connecticut Agricultural Experiment Station, there is cyanide in my silver cleaner, and my oranges have been rouged with coal-tar dyes. My steam iron spurts hot water from the fill hole, my food-waste disposer doesn't chew corn husks properly, my phonograph is giddy with wow, flutter, rumble, and hum. Acid water slowly eats away the glossy finish on my sinks, lavatories, tubs, and what it does to the owner himself no man can say. My double-glazed windows are subject to between-pane condensation, and moths and carpet beetles are at work inside the hammers of my piano. My 3-hp. rotary snowthrower is a bust. "Snow was ejected as a powdery mist, which blew back on the operator," the *Annual* says, and this proved to be the case; when I returned from the trial run I resembled a Lapp. Unthrown snow drifts now about my automobile, my apple trees, and Candace, who has gone out to collect the mail. But let her go, for I am writing letters, wrothy letters, to the manufacturer, the Federal Trade Commission, the National Better Business Bureau, and the Attorney General of the state of New York, as the *Annual* advises me to do. The world is sagging, snagging, scaling, spalling, pilling, pinging, pitting, warping, checking, fading, chipping, cracking, yellowing, leaking, staling, shrinking, and in dynamic unbalance, and there is mildew to think about, and ruptures and fractures of internal organs from lap belts, and substandard brake fluids, and plastic pipes alluring to rats, and transistor radios whose estimated battery life, like the life of man, is a feeble, flickering thing.

Candace dear, heart of my heart, take your hand off that package of fabric softener! It may produce an insoluble curd, and you wouldn't want that, would you? "The biggest problem the consumer has in selecting shoes is not fashion, though that may be his first consideration, but selecting a shoe that will not ultimately lead to the distortion of his foot." And don't forget about shirts that develop a yellow tint! And thermal flame-resistant underwear—especially quilted polyester fiber-nylon shell suits—which, once ignited, melts to form a burning, sticky, adhering plastic! And paint failure! And pie mixes laced with esters, ethers, and aldehydes of undefined character! And bicycles with poor pedal design! And dimensionally-unstable rayon blankets! And electronic organs that make popping sounds! And coffee mills that adversely affect the flavor of the beverage! And travel irons whose soleplates blister! And desk fans with high noise levels! And electric shavers with tendency to irritate neck! Recall, too, that purchasing a camera, whether new or used, can be a risky operation for the uninitiated! That few diamonds are entirely free from every sort of defect or flaw! That with today's watches a fairly high price gives no assurance of reliable performance or durable construction! That tire-gauge designs leave much to be desired! And, finally, that the custom of going around without a hat or shirt in hot sunny climates, and allowing children to do so, should be strongly discouraged!

O brave *Consumer Bulletin Annual,* holding the line in a world where the best lack all conviction, while the worst are full of passionate intensity! You give me touchstones with which to protect myself against the deceptive pricing, false gift offers, spurious claims, bait advertising, and general rascality of the American economy. "A good spring should be noiseless, or comparatively so. Push on it in quiet surroundings." Of course. Do you mind if I take this spring into the elevator with me for a moment? And close the doors, will you, floorwalker? And what are you grinning about? "For durability, loops of a terry towel should be thickly packed and firm. Check firmness by inserting a pin into a pile loop, raising it up from the towel slightly." Pin poised, I advance into the murky depths of the towel store, clearly a man with a mission. In the department store, I stand bent over a portable refrigerator, inspecting a tray of ice cubes with my jeweler's loupe. Yes, it has taken them much too long to freeze. Quickly I unfasten the jesses that bind Hugo, the killer hawk, to my wrist. Dubious refrigeration shall not go unpunished! Now Hugo is aloft, heading for Panda, Iowa, where the worthless devices are manufactured. See him soar!

And now Port Moresby. Come, Candace, let me coax you out from under that bell jar, into which you have repaired to guard delicate ears against sound of china crazing in the kitchen. Come, Candace, and don't worry about the packing. The only appliance I plan to take with me is Hugo.

Letters to the Editore

The Editor of Shock Art *has hardly to say that the amazing fecundity of the LeDuff–Galerie Z controversy during the past five numbers has enflamed both shores of the Atlantic, at intense length. We did not think anyone would care, but apparently, a harsh spot has been touched. It is a terrible trouble to publish an international art-journal in two languages simultaneously, and the opportunities for dissonance have not been missed. We will accept solely one more correspondence on this matter, addressed to our editorial offices, 6, Viale Berenson, 20144 Milano (Italy), and that is the end. Following is a poor selection of the recent reverberations.*

Nicolai PONT
Editore

SIRS:

This is to approximate a reply to the reply of Doug LeDuff to our publicity of 29 December which appeared in your journal and raised such possibilities of anger. The

9

fumings of Mr. LeDuff were not unanticipated by those who know. However nothing new has been proved by these vapourings, which leave our points untouched, for the most part, and limp off into casuistry and vague threats. We are not very intimidated! The matters of substantial interest in our original publicity are scathless. Mr. LeDuff clearly has the opinion that the readers of *Shock Art* are dulls, which we do not. Our contention that the work of Mr. LeDuff the American are sheer copyings of the work of our artist Gianbello Bruno can be sustained by ruthless scholarship, of the type that Mr. LeDuff cannot, for obvious reasons, bear to produce. But the recipient of today's art-scene is qualified enough to judge for himself. We need only point to the 1958 exposition at the Galerie Berger, Paris, in which the "asterisk" series of Bruno was first inserted, to see what is afoot. The American makes the claim that he has been painting asterisks since 1955—we say, if so, where are these asterisks? In what collections? In what expositions? With what documentation? Whereas the accomplishment of the valuable Bruno is fully documented, by the facts and other printed materials, as was brought out in our original publicity. That LeDuff has infiltrated the collectors of four continents with his importunity proves nothing, so much so as to be dismissive and final.

Of course the fully American attitude of the partisans of LeDuff, that there is nothing except America, is evident here in the apparently fair evaluation of the protagonists which is in fact deeply biased in the direction of their native land. The manifestation of Mr. Ringwood Paul in your most recent number, wherein he points out (correctly) that the asterisks of LeDuff are six-pointed versus the asterisks of Bruno which have uniformly five points, is not a "knock-out blow." In claiming severe plastic originality for LeDuff on this score, Mr. Paul only displays the thickness of entrenched opinion. It is easy, once one has "borrowed" a concept from another artist, to add a little small improvement, but it is not so easy to put it back again without anyone noticing! Finally, the assertion of the estimable critic (American again, we understand!) Paula Marx that the moiré effect achieved by both Bruno and LeDuff by the superimposition of many asterisks on many other asterisks is an advancement created by LeDuff alone and then adduced by Bruno, is flatly false. Must we use carbon-dating on these recent peintures to establish truth, as if we were archeologists faced with an exhausted culture? No, there are living persons among us who remember. To support this affair with references to the "idealism" of the œuvre of LeDuff is the equivalent of saying, "Yes, mostly his shirts are clean." But the clean shirt of LeDuff conceals that which can only throw skepticism on this œuvre.

Bernardo BROWN
H. L. AKEFELDT
Galerie Z
Milan

SIRS:

The whole thing is to make me smile. What do these Americans want? They come over here and everyone installs them in the best hotels with lavish napery, but still, complaints of every kind. Profiting unduly from the attentions of rich bourgeois, they then emplane once again

for America, richer and thoughtful of coming again to
again despoil our bourgeois. Doug LeDuff is a pig and a
child, but so are his enemies.

Pino VITT
Rome

CARO NIKKI—

May I point out the facility of the LeDuff–Galerie Z
debate that you have allowed to discolor your pages for
many months now? Whether or not you were admirable
in your decision to accept for publication the Galerie Z
advertisings defaming LeDuff (whom I personally feel to
be a monger of dampish wallpaper) is not for me to state,
although you were clearly incredible, good faith notwith-
standing. I can only indicate, from the womb of history,
that both LeDuff and Bruno have impersonated the ac-
complishments of the Magdeburg Handwerker (May 14,
1938).

Hugo TIMME
Düsseldorf

SIRS:

The members of the SURFACE Group (Basel) are unfal-
teringly supportive of the immense America master,
Doug LeDuff.

Gianni ARNAN
Michel PIK
Zin REGALE
Erik ZORN
Basel

EDITORE (if any)
Shock Art
MILANO

The most powerful international interests of the gallery-critic-collector cartel have only to gain by the obfuscations of the LeDuff–Galerie Z bickerings. How come you have ignored Elaine Grasso, whose work of now many years in the field of parentheses is entirely propos?

Magda BAUM
Rotterdam

SIRS:

Shock Art is being used unforeseeably in this affair. The asterisk has a long provenance and is neither the formulation of LeDuff nor of Bruno either, in any case. The asterisk (from the Greek *asteriskos* or small star) presents itself in classical mythology as the sign which Hera, enraged by yet another of Zeus's manifold infidelities, placed on the god's brow while he slept, to remind him when he gazed in the mirror in the morning that he should be somewhere else. I plead with you, Sig. Pont, to publish my letter, so that people will know.

G. PHILIOS
Athens

CARO PONT,

It was kind of you to ask me to comment on the good fight you are making in your magazine. A poor critic is not often required to consult on these things, even though he may have much better opinions than those who are standing in the middle, because of his long and

careful training in ignoring the fatigues of passionate in-
volvement—if he has it!

Therefore, calmly and without prejudice toward either
party, let us examine the issues with an unruffled eye.
LeDuff's argument (in *Shock Art* #37) that an image, once
floated on the international art-sea, is a fish that anyone
may grab with impunity, and make it his own, would not
persuade an oyster. Questions of primacy are not to be
scumbled in this way, which, had he been writing from a
European perspective, he would understand, and be
ashamed. The brutality of the American rape of the
world's exhibition spaces and organs of art-information
has distanciated his senses. The historical aspects have
been adequately trodden by others, but there is one cate-
gory yet to be entertained—that of the psychological. The
fact that LeDuff is replicated in every museum, in every
journal, that one cannot turn one's gaze without bumping
into this raw plethora, LeDuff, LeDuff, LeDuff (whereas
poor Bruno, the true progenitor, is eating the tops of
bunches of carrots)—what has this done to LeDuff himself? It has turned him into a dead artist, but the corpse
yet bounces in its grave, calling attentions toward itself in
the most unseemly manner. But truth cannot be swallowed forever. When the real story of low optical stimulus
is indited, Bruno will be rectified.

Titus Toselli DOLLA
Palermo

That Cosmopolitan Girl

Must a girl always be protected by a man? Not this girl! When I lived in California I sometimes picked a man up in *my* car for a date if his was in the garage, loaned to a friend or—my car was in better shape! (No, he wasn't emasculated and we stayed friends.) Last week at J.F.K. I carried one of *Stephen*'s bags. He was loaded with golf clubs and I only had a garment bag and a Vuitton. (No, I *didn't* throw my back out and Stephen and I are still together!) Isn't it silly to try to preserve old clichés when naturalness and freedom are so much better?

—*Adv. for* Cosmopolitan *in* The N.Y. Times.

Of course the next day when <u>Stephen</u> picked me up for dinner at Vuitton, looking <u>hysterically</u> handsome in his Vuitton coveralls, I was a shade taken aback when he literally <u>demanded</u> that I pay for the cab. (He always used to do little things like that as a matter of course!) Well, I paid cheerfully, because I have this magazine I read that teaches me how to be <u>natural</u> and <u>healthy</u> and <u>resilient</u>, but then when we got out of the cab he <u>loaded</u> this <u>immense</u> steamer trunk on my back. I said, "<u>Stephen</u>, what are you <u>doing</u>?" He said, "Just get it inside, dollbaby." Well, I don't know

15

if you've ever marched into Vuitton with a
Vuitton steamer trunk on your back, huffing and
puffing and bent half double, but I can tell
you <u>this</u>, it makes you feel kind of <u>weird</u>. But
I <u>coped</u>—I just pretended I was some kind of
super-soigné woman <u>mover</u>! (It's <u>silly</u> to
preserve the old clichés about roles and such
when <u>naturalness</u> and <u>freedom</u> and <u>health</u> are so
much better but this time I <u>did</u> throw my back
out!) We got a good table in spite of the
steamer trunk because <u>Stephen</u> has this absolutely
<u>wizardly</u> way with the V. headwaiters, and we
ordered our own very special-together drink,
nitroglycerin and soda (because of Stephen's
really absolutely <u>unique</u> heart condition—he's
the only person in the <u>whole</u> <u>world</u> who has it!),
and I was beginning to feel all glow-y and
comfortable, except that my back was positively
<u>ruined</u>, because of carrying the steamer trunk.
"Why are you twitching like that?" Stephen
asked (a tiny bit crossly, I thought) and I
explained to him that my back hurt. Usually he
is the living <u>soul</u> of <u>compassion</u>—really <u>sweet</u>—
but this time all he said was "If you didn't
spend all your time reading that damned
<u>magazine</u>, and <u>italicizing</u> every third word in
your sentences, you'd have a <u>strong</u>, <u>healthy</u>
back, just like your mother did. I'm going to
get you a <u>washtub</u> and a wash<u>board</u> for your
birthday. I bet you don't even know what a
washboard <u>looks</u> like. I bet you never even saw
one outside of a <u>jug</u> <u>band</u>." (I thought that
bit about my <u>italicizing</u> words was a bit
<u>cruel</u>, because <u>he</u> does it <u>too</u>—all the <u>time</u>!)

But I just gave him a quick grin and an impish,
sort of <u>California</u> look, and asked if I could
have another N & S. "You picking up the bloody
<u>tab</u>?" he asked, a teeny bit viciously, I
thought. But then I remembered that <u>men</u> have
their little moods, just like women, and that
<u>Stephen</u> is in very heavy trouble at the
<u>office</u> right now, due to that nasty S.E.C.
investigation, just because he tipped off a
couple of hundred clients about the receivership
ahead of time, but for heaven's sake, he was
just trying to be <u>loyal</u> to his <u>friends</u>. So I
just said offhandedly, "Sure." But then he
reached over and began to unlatch the steamer
trunk, which was still standing by the table,
and I noticed that all the waiters and captains
and <u>busboys</u> had begun to gather around, to see
what was <u>inside</u>! (I guess their curiosity was
normal and healthy and lovable, but it made me
feel just the least most microcosmic bit <u>itchy</u>!)
And what <u>was</u> inside you would never fathom in
a thousand years! It was <u>another</u> <u>woman</u>! "Get
up," Stephen said to me. "This is Elberta and
I want to sit next to her." Well, I almost
crumbled into <u>matchsticks</u>, as you can <u>imagine</u>,
but I just acted <u>natural</u> as hard as I could,
and that was easier because she was <u>wearing</u> the
most peculiar <u>creation</u> you could possibly
conjure up in your wildest dreams—I think it's
called a <u>housedress</u>. I nearly <u>died</u> laughing,
inside of course (outside I was still being
natural and healthy, even though my back was
giving me <u>pure</u> <u>unshirted</u> <u>hell</u>), and even smiled
at the thought that my carrying the steamer

trunk into the restaurant on my back hadn't
emasculated Stephen <u>one</u> <u>little</u> <u>bit</u>—as a matter
of fact he was sort of <u>feeling</u> Elberta's
handbag, which looked like it was made of an
old armadillo shell or something, in a manner
that was downright <u>lascivious</u>. Well, I must
admit that I was in the most <u>infinitesimal</u> bit
of a twit, so I dipped into my Vuitton and
brought out my copy of the current issue of
the magazine to see if the advice columns had
anything <u>à propos</u>, if there was any strong,
natural, <u>lovable</u> way to deal with this rather
<u>hideous</u> situation, but all of the writers
seemed to be <u>preoccupied</u> with the problems of
unmarried mothers this month, and that wasn't
my problem, and <u>Stephen</u> was talking with
Elberta in low tones that I couldn't hear,
although I tried, so I reached over and patted
Elberta on the hand, the hand that was curled
around one of <u>our</u> drinks, and asked her in the
<u>nicest</u> possible way what magazine she read,
what magazine she identified with, what magazine
<u>defined</u> her, because of course I was <u>insanely</u>
curious about how she achieved that really
<u>phony</u> wholesomeness that she <u>exuded</u> all over
Stephen like a <u>web</u> or something. She just looked
at me and said, "<u>Scientific American</u>, dearie."

Eugénie Grandet

Balzac's novel *Eugénie Grandet* was published in 1833. Grandet, a rich miser, has an only child, Eugénie. She falls in love with her young cousin, Charles. When she learns he is financially ruined, she lends him her savings. Charles goes to the West Indies, secretly engaged to marry Eugénie on his return. Years go by. Grandet dies and Eugénie becomes an heiress. But Charles, ignorant of her wealth, writes to ask her for his freedom: he wants to marry a rich girl. Eugénie releases him, pays his father's debts, and marries without love an old friend of the family, Judge de Bonfons.

—*The Thesaurus of Book Digests*

"Oh, oh, where's Old Grandet going so early in the morning, running as though his house were on fire?"

"He'll end up by buying the whole town of Saumur!"

"He doesn't even notice the cold, his mind is always on his business!"

"Everything he does is significant!"

"He knows the secrets and mysteries of the life and death of money!"

•

"It looks as though I'm going to be quite successful here in Saumur," thought Charles, unbuttoning his coat.

•

A great many people are interested in the question: Who will obtain Eugénie Grandet's hand?

•

Eugénie Grandet's hand:

•

Judge de Bonfons arrives carrying flowers.

•

"Mother, have you noticed that this society we're in tends to be a little . . . repressive?"

"What does that mean, Eugénie? What does that mean, that strange new word, 'repressive,' that I have never heard before?"

"It means . . . it's like when you decide to do something, and you get up out of your chair to do it, and you take a step, and then become aware of frosty glances being directed at you from every side."

"Frosty glances?"

"Your desires are stifled."

"What desires are you talking about?"

"Just desires in general. Any desires. It's a whole . . . I guess atmosphere is the word . . . a tendency on the part of the society . . ."

"You'd better sew some more pillow cases, Eugénie."

•

Part of a letter:

> . . . And now he's ruined, a
> friends will desert him, and
> humiliation. Oh, I wish I ha
> straight to heaven, where his
> but this is madness . . . I re
> that of Charles.
>   I have sent him to you so
> news of my death to him and
> in store for him. Be a father to ·
> not tear him away from his
> would kiss him. I beg him on m
> which, as his mother's heir, he
> But this is a superfluous ple
> will realize that he must not
> Persuade him to give up all his
> time comes. Reveal to him th
> which he must live from now
> still has any love for me, tell
> not lost for him. Yes, work, wh
> give him back the fortune I ha
> And if he is willing to listen
> who for his sake would like to

•

"Please allow me to retire," Charles said. "I must begin
a long and sad correspondence."

"Certainly, nephew."

•

"The painter is here from Paris!"

"Good day, painter. What is your name?"

"My name, sir, is John Graham!"

"John Graham! That is not a French name!"

"No, sir. I am an American. My dates are 1881–1961."

"Well, you have an air of competence. Is that your
equipment there, on the stagecoach platform?"

"Yes. That is my equipment. That is my easel, my palette, and my paint box containing tins of paints as well as the finest camel's-hair brushes. In this bag, here, are a few changes of clothes, for I anticipate that this portrait will take several days."

"Well, that is fine. How do you like our country?"

"It appears to be a very fine country. I imagine a lot of painting could get done in this country."

"Yes, we have some pretty good painters of our own. That is why I am· surprised to find that they sent an American painter, rather than a French one, to do Mlle. Eugénie's portrait. But I'm sure you will do a first-class job. We're paying you enough."

"Yes, the fee is quite satisfactory."

"Have you brought any examples of your work, so we can see what kind of thing you do?"

"Well, in this album here . . . this is a portrait of Ellen West . . . this one is Mrs. Margot Heap . . . that's an Indian chief . . . that's Patsy Porker . . ."

"Why are they all cross-eyed?"

"Well, that's just the way I do it. I don't see anything wrong with that. It often occurs in nature."

"But *every one* is . . ."

"Well, what's so peculiar about that? I just like . . . that's just the way I do it. I *like* . . ."

•

"In my opinion, Eugénie wasn't fondled enough as a child."

"Adolphe des Grassins wasn't fondled enough either!"

"And Judge de Bonfons?"

"Who could bring himself to fondle Judge de Bonfons!"

"And Charles Grandet?"

"His history in this regard is not known. But it has been observed that he is forever *patting himself,* pat pat pat, on the hair, on the kneecap, pat pat pat pat pat pat. This implies—"

"These children need fondling!"

"The state should fondle these poor children!"

"Balzac himself wasn't fondled enough!"

"Men are fools!"

•

Eugénie Grandet with ball:

•

Charles and Eugénie understand each other.

They speak only with their eyes.

The poor ruined dandy withdraws into a corner and remains there in calm, proud silence.

But from time to time his cousin's gentle, caressing glance

•

"No more butter, Eugénie. You've already used up a whole half pound this month."

"But, Father . . . the butter for Charles's éclair!"

•

Butter butter

•

Eugénie Grandet decides to kill her father.

•

Charles decides to try his luck in the Indies—that deadliest of climates.

•

"Here, Charles, take this money of mine. This money that my father gave me. This money that if he finds out I gave it to you, all hell will break loose. I want you to have it, to finance your operations in the Indies—that deadliest of climates."

"No, Eugénie, I couldn't do that. I couldn't take your money. No, I won't do it. No."

"No, I mean it, Charles. Take the money and use it for worthy purposes. Please. See, here is a ducat, minted in 1756 and still bright as day. And here are some doubloons, worth two escudos each. And here are some shiny

quadroons, of inestimable value. And here in this bag are
thalers and bobs, and silver quids and copper bawbees.
Altogether, nearly six thousand francs. Take it, it's
yours."

"No, Eugénie, I can't take your money. I can't do it."

"No, Charles, take my money. My little hoard."

"O.K."

•

In order not to interrupt the course of events which
took place within the Grandet family, we must now
glance ahead at the operations which the old man carried
out in Paris by means of the des Grassins. A month after
the banker's departure, Grandet was in possession of
enough government stock, purchased at eighty francs a
share, to yield him an income of a hundred thousand
francs a year. The information given after his death by
the inventory of his property never threw the slightest
light on the means by which his wary mind conceived to
exchange the price of the certificate for the certificate itself. Monsieur Cruchot believed that Nanon had unwit-
tingly been the trusty instrument by which the money was
delivered. It was at about that time that she went away for
five days on the pretext of putting something in order at
Froidfond, as though the old man were capable of leaving anything in disorder!

With regard to the affairs of the house of Guillaume
Grandet, all the old man's expectations were realized. As
is well known, the Bank of France has precise information on all the large fortunes of Paris and the provinces.
The names of des Grassins and Félix Grandet of Saumur
were well known there and enjoyed the respect granted
to all noted financial figures whose wealth is based on
enormous holdings of unmortgaged land. The arrival of

the banker from Saumur, who was said to be under orders to liquidate, for the sake of honor, the house of Grandet in Paris, was therefore enough to spare the deceased merchant's memory the shame of protested notes. The seals were broken in the presence of the creditors, who

•

"Here's a million and a half francs, Judge," Eugénie said, drawing from her bosom a certificate for a hundred shares in the Bank of France.

•

Charles in the Indies. He sold:

    Chinese
    Negroes
    swallows' nests
    children
    artists

•

Photograph of Charles in the Indies:

•

The letter:

DEAR COUSIN,
  I have decided to marry a Mlle. d'Aubrion, and
not you. Her nose turns red, under certain circum-
stances: but I have contrived a way of not looking at
her, at those times—all will be well. If my children
are to get into the École Normale, the marriage is es-
sential; and we have to live for the children, don't
we? A brilliant life awaits me, is what I am trying to
say to you, if I don't marry you, and that is why I am
marrying this other girl, who is hideously ugly but
possessed of a notable, if decayed, position in the ar-
istocracy. Therefore those binding promises we
exchanged, on the bench, are, to all intents and purposes, mooted. If I have smothered your hopes at
the same time, what can I do? We get the destiny we
deserve, and I have done so many evil things, in the
Indies, that I am no longer worthy of you, probably.
Knowing chuckles will doubtless greet this news, the
news of my poor performance, in Saumur—I ask you
to endure them, for the sake of
                                  Your formerly loving,
                                  Charles

•

"I have decided to give everything to the Church."
"An income of eight hundred thousand a year!"
"Yes."
"It will kill your father."
"You think it will kill him if I give everything to the
Church?"
"I certainly do."
"Run and fetch the curé this instant."

•

Old Grandet clutches his chest, and capitulates. Eight hundred thousand a year! He gasps. A death by gasping.

•

Adolphe des Grassins, an unsuccessful suitor of Eugénie Grandet, follows his father to Paris. He becomes a worthless scoundrel there.

Snap Snap

"Such a claim is ridiculous," Quynh snapped . . . (*Time*, June 4)

. . . Rusk snapped, "I don't know how one draws the line . . ." (*Time*, June 4)

Snapped Canadian Heavyweight George Chuvalo: "It's a phony, a real phony." (*Time*, June 4)

Harvard Law School Professor Charles Haar snapped . . . (*Time*, June 4)

"We're not playing Mickey Mouse with this thing," snapped Christoper Kraft, Gemini 4's mission director. (*Time*, June 11)

Barry [Goldwater] snapped: "Frankly, I don't know enough about John Lindsay to give you the time of day." (*Newsweek*, June 14)

. . . snapped London's *Economist*. (*Newsweek*, June 14)

"I don't have to wait for revelation to know that I am the natural head in Nigeria," snaps [Mormon Anie Dick] Obot . . . (*Time*, June 18)

"Ridiculous!" snapped Hollywood's Peter Lawford . . . (*Newsweek*, June 21)

"Goddammit, Bundy," snapped the President, "I've told you that when I want you I'll call you." (*Time*, June 25)

"Adolescent," snapped Author Ralph Ellison. (*Time*, June 25)

Snapped [Walter] Hallstein: "The obstinate maintaining of divisive internal antagonisms could make Europe the Balkans of the world." (*Time*, June 25)

Americans are "abominable," [Lord] Russell snapped . . . (*Time*, June 25)

"Oh, you have, have you?" snapped [Professor Daniel] Berman. (*Time*, July 2)

[Algerian Official Spokesman Si] Slimane snapped . . . (*Time*, July 2)

[Peking Foreign Minister] Chen Yi snapped: "That's not serious." (*Newsweek*, July 12)

Snapped one M.P.: "Philip is a very highly paid civil servant . . . who is expected to keep his nose out of politics." (*Time*, July 16)

Snapped Kenya's Foreign Minister Joseph Murumbi . . . (*Newsweek*, July 19)

In another speech he [Ludwig Erhard] snapped that . . . (*Time*, July 23)

Snapped Spahn: "First, I'm a pitcher. Then I'm a coach." (*Time*, July 23)

"A complete diplomatic sellout," snapped a conservative. (*Newsweek*, July 26)

[Robert] Kennedy snapped: "I'm shocked . . ." (*Newsweek*, July 26)

"I want you," snapped the President. "Bring Mrs. Goldberg right over to the office." (*Time*, July 30)

The difficulty is with my style. That much is clear. My style pure, unadulterated mouse. Mouse all the way. Gray movements along the baseboards of corridors of power. When what is wanted is mouse*trap* style. Snap-snap. Trigger-quick. Incisive. Decisive. Snapper knows what's what. Lashes out. Got the facts. Tip of the tongue. Snap-snap.

Twenty-three years in Bureau of Hatcheries and what to show for it? Nothing. Not a thing. Since that day in 1944 when they entrusted me with the pike. *Clitterhouse,* they said, *a chance to show what you can do.* And then decades of neglect. A GS-10 with no hope of 11. Not even allowed a framed photograph of the President for my wall. Make do with framed photograph of little beagle. Because I am soft-spoken. Because I am slow to anger. Because I mull, think through. What has it got me? Watery sauerkraut in the cafeteria every Wednesday. Eyes-only memos passing me by. The pike respect me, perhaps. How is one to know?

Perhaps even now it is not too late. Change style. Learn to snap. Leave government service, plunge into jungles of commerce. Then one day surface in the pages of *Time,* for instance, where I am seen to be doing my job with spectacular competence: "For shareholders of giant U.S. Python, long one of the hemisphere's three top-rated producers of industrial snake musculature, there was good news last week: engorgement of two-hundred-year-old Pantages Plantfood, Inc., flourishing Chilean phosphorus concern. Acquisition of Pantages will give Python, already active in Christmas cards, calorie counters, and cut glass, a stranglehold on the booming international fishmeal market, solidly enhance its sly sidestep into rub-

ber overshoes (through fast-climbing International
Buckle, Java-based subsidiary whose 1964 year-end
profits totaled $2.5 million). Behind the move was U.S.
Python's shrewd, snappish Charles Clitterhouse III,
forty-four, who came to Python three years ago after a
hitch with Midwest Trace & Bit. Clitterhouse, a loner who
scorns computers ('window dressing!' he snapped on one
occasion) and programs the entire Python operation in
his head, has guided the once-ailing colossus back to
health with an unorthodox combination of brains, drive,
and peevishness. 'Asperity,' he snaps, 'is the key to
greater profits in the current economic climate,' and sten-
cils the company motto ('Mala Gratia') on Python trucks,
water coolers, and junior executives. An exotic who lives
in a bank vault with his three wives, one child, Clitterhouse relaxes on rare days off by trading tartnesses
with a few close friends, snapping Polaroid photos of
company installations. 'Let the other guy be civil,' snaps
he, 'I'll . . .' "

But this is fantasy, Clitterhouse. The problem remains.
How to impinge upon consciousness of superiors? How
to reach hearing aids of the mighty? Cry and warn. And
urge. The newsweeklies a cacophony of crying and warning, and urging. Not just snapping. Rounded Top Person
style includes snapping, crying, warning, urging. Vigor.
The raised voice. No murmurers need apply.

Consider the month of June. Syrian Strongman Amin
Hafez cried that Egyptian Strongman Gamal Abdel Nas-
ser was soft on Israel. "Cried Hafez: 'What is he waiting
for?'" (*Time,* June 11) Brazilian Politico Carlos Lacerda
cried that Brazilian Economics Minister Roberto Campos

was soft in head. " 'Campos,' cried Lacerda, is 'a mental weakling . . .' " (*Time,* June 11) Dominican Insurgent Colonel Francisco Caamaño Deñó cried that elections for his strife-torn country were out of the question. " 'First,' cried Caamaño, 'the revolution's goal must be fulfilled. After that we can talk about elections.' " (*Time,* June 11) Cuban Strongman Fidel Castro cried that this was a decisive year. " 'This was a decisive year,' cried Castro." (*Time,* June 18) Strongman Castro cried again (*Time,* June 25), discussing whereabouts of Henchman Che Guevara. " 'If the Americans are puzzled,' cried Castro . . . , 'let them remain puzzled.' " Strongman Castro nearly always cries in newsweeklies. Sometimes roars. Has been heard to snort. But mostly cries.

Others cry too. Humorist Harry Hershfield cried (*Time,* June 25). "O.K., cried Hershfield, so maybe [New York City Council President and Mayoral Candidate and Strongman Paul R.] Screvane is of Italian-Irish descent and married to Limerick-born Bridie McKessy—but 'he has a Jewish heart.' " An extended cry. Dominican Politico Rafael Tavera cried ("There will not be peace until the last invader is destroyed and the last Yankee property is seized"). An army general cried ("I thought you were going to play all the instruments, Mr. President"). Theodore Roosevelt cried ("By Jove! I'll have to do something for that young man"). Marcel Carné cried (*"Parties!"*). British Bridge Expert Ralph Swimer cried. Joseph Tronzo, sports editor of Beaver Falls, Pa., *News-Tribune,* cried. An old lady cried. Old pensioners cried. A Ferrari mechanic cried.

And there were warnings. Conservative French Novelist Michel de Saint Pierre warned ("We encounter Marxist

infiltration at every step in our Christian lives"). Caamaño
warned. Campos warned. Many economists warned. Mel-
ler & Co.'s John Amico warned darkly ("Smart money is
leaving the market"). One Washington policymaker
warned. And urgings. Sargent Shriver urged. The President urged. Senator Fulbright urged.

Clitterhouse, do you get the message? Pay attention to
speech. Basically, you're not a bad fellow, but you have
this terrible habit of . . . *saying* everything. Don't *say*.
Snap, cry, urge, warn. Otherwise you stand in grave
danger of being thought a relic of nineteenth century, a
muted cough along the tapped wire of history.

Consider July. July, in newsweeklies, a shrill, clamor-
ous, fateful month, cantanker, distemper everywhere,
snappings, cryings, urgings, warnings. French Foreign
Minister Couve de Murville cried ("Too much has been
asked of France!"). Disc Jockey Murray the K cried
("Sarge, baby, you're a real swinger"). Missouri Democrat
Paul Jones cried ("This is the damnedest thing I've seen
in all my life"). Critics of India's Prime Minister Shastri
cried ("sellout"). Painter Marc Chagall cried ("Divorce!").
British Deputy Prime Minister George Brown cried. Canadian Opposition Leader John Diefenbaker cried.
Roger Rappenceau cried. Pakistan's President Ayub took
up the cry. The Democrats cried. Walter Hallstein cried.
Painter Bernard Buffet cried twice, once in *Time* ("*Au
secours!*" July 16), once in *Newsweek* (something to the effect that a Swede was cutting up his refrigerator, July 19).
Philosopher George Picht warned. British Chancellor of
the Exchequer James Callaghan ("among others")
warned. The President warned. White House and State
Department spokesmen warned. The pastor of Cologne's

powerful St. Ursula's Church warned. Brookfield (Ill.) Zoo authorities warned. Dodger Physician Dr. Robert Kerlan warned. CORE's James Farmer warned. U Thant warned. Robert Kennedy warned. Boumedienne warned. Papandreou warned. The government of Sarawak urged. *Clitterhouse, can you hear me? Open wide, Clitterhouse, open wide!*

The Angry Young Man

The angry young man jumps over the lazy dog's back

Four thousand pieces of second-class mail! Four thousand pieces of second-class mail enriched with certain letters of historical importance and literary forgeries of great cunning! These cover the goatskin rug. The goatskin rug covers the lazy dog. The angry young man, using the new fiberglass pole, makes his run, jumps! He is aloft, he is up in the air, he has cleared the lazy dog, the goatskin rug, the four thousand pieces of second-class mail! A new earth record for the lazy dog's back jump!

What a wonderful thing it is to be angry! To be young.

What the dictionary says

an'gry young' man, 1. (*often cap.*) one of a group of British writers since the late 1950's whose works reflect

strong dissatisfaction with, frustration by, and rebellion against tradition and society. 2. any author writing in this manner. 3. any frustrated, rebellious person. Also, referring to a woman, **an′gry young/ wom′an.**
　　　　　—Random House Dictionary of the English Language

His opinion of the Queen
　　"She's as comely as a cow in a cage."

His clothing
　　Brown corduroy pants, black turtleneck sweater, work shoes, coonskin cap, glass of porter in right hand. Or, dark-blue suit, black shoes, white shirt, maroon tie—this worn when receiving the O.B.E. or other honors.

Opinion of the present situation
　　"What is your opinion of the present situation?"
　　"Well, it's better than sleeping with a dead policeman."

Before the mirror
　　The dark muscle of the angry young man, surrounded as it is by the light muscle, flexes.
　　"Mirror, mirror, on the wall, who's the most baddest angry young man of all?"

Attitude toward the Revolution
　　"Well, it can't happen here, can it? I mean, Daddy won't allow it, will he? Daddy and his pals, and the posh papers, the whole rotten lot of them? I mean, it's just a lot of cock, now, isn't it?"

Taxes paid Inland Revenue for the year 1959
　　£ 2,850.

The angry young man meets the angry young woman
  "Tom!"
  "Helen!"
  "How've you been? Angry?"
  "Rabid."
  "Good girl. Tea?"
  "Yes thanks I'd love some."

Moment of self-doubt in the psychic life of the angry young man
  "Is there any point in being an angry *old* man?"

The Albert Hall lecture
  "Yes. Well. My subject tonight is cooking before marriage. It has been my observation, and I'm not alone in
this, other people have made the same observation, a
blind man could see it, that the young people today are
doing a bloody great lot of *cooking together before marriage.*
Cooking together, shamelessly, night after night, and
God knows I'm no prude but the sight of these young
. . . *lovebirds* . . . without so much as a by-your-leave,
without so much as the shred of a marriage contract between them, well it's a bit much now isn't it . . . wallow-
ing in . . . *spices* . . . rosemary . . . saffron . . ."

Passing of time in the life of the angry young man
  L(%¢, L(%&, L(%*, L(%(, L(¢), L(¢L, L(¢@, L(¢#,
L(¢$, L(¢%, L(¢¢, L(¢&, L(¢*, L(¢(, L(&), L(&L, L(&@,
L(&#, L(&$

Characteristics of the angry young book
  The angry young book should be a good true book of a
familiar and reliable pattern. It should concern itself with
human emotions of standard issue plus at least one (1)

nonstandard emotion for seasoning and piquancy. It
should extend to a good number of pages and said pages
should hold a full body of printing both recto and verso,
the lines so arranged as to come out even at the right-
hand margin, save at the termination of paragraphs and
the like. It should have a good true spine to which the
pages are attached by sewing and a strong glue, and no
page should fly out of the whole save by prior arrangement, as when the author is especially angry. The same
should reflect strong dissatisfaction with, frustration by,
and rebellion against tradition and society. The book
should, ideally, burn the hands—a third-degree burn.

*Current manifestations of the "kitchen sink" school of British
painting, thought at one time to be analogous to the work of the
angry young men*
    There are none.

The angry young man attends the Annual Meeting
    At the Annual Meeting, voices are raised in anger. The
hall is crawling with coonskin caps, which are waved, or
dropped, or flung. Large wheyfaced angry young men
grapple with small wiry angry young men—the faces of
the latter are made of string. The chairman calls for
order but in vain; order is not wanted here. Skiffle bands
engage in cutting contests. The floor is black with spilled
porter and bile. Individual angry young men stand at
various points with their backs to the crowd playing trum-
pets or cornets—each is playing a different tune. Other
angry young men are refusing to speak to other angry
young men. The flag is trampled, spat upon, urinated
upon, used as a bar rag. Harrod's is burned in effigy as it

is every year (but some angry young men are seen snatching candied yummies from the flames).

Nevertheless, important theoretical questions are raised:

1. Is fresh ever-renewed soaring searing good-quality anger possible?

2. How long, expressed in decades, can true anger be maintained without modulating into, say, pique?

3. Was it *originally* pique, made to seem anger by skilled dramaturgy?

4. What can be learned by studies of the shelf life of the average volcano?

5. Can anger be institutionalized, can it avoid being institutionalized, and what is the place in all this of the cup of tea?

6. Does the boiling point of the cup of tea vary from corrupt society to corrupt society?

Whereabouts of the wives of the angry young man

The wives of the angry young man are now married to other people—doctors, mostly.

The movement of history

The movement of history is heavy, and slow. The movement of history always takes place *behind one's back*. As your gaze is fixed upon something immediately in front of you—the object of your anger, for example—history makes a slight, almost imperceptible slither, or shudder, in a direction of its own choice. The distinguishing mark of this direction is that it is not the one that you had anticipated. How history manages this is not known. Because history is made of the will of all individuals taken together, because these oceans of individuals are mostly, or always, in conflict, the movement of history is at one and the same time tightly bound, and outrageous. The problem may be diagrammed in the following way:

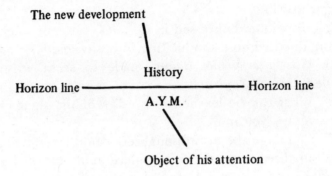

Study of the previous behavior of history does not prepare one for these shifts, which are discomfiting in the extreme. Nothing prepares you.

Ultimate meaning of the angry young man

The ultimate meaning of the angry young man is not known. What is known is the shape of his greatest fear— that all of his efforts, from learning to speak to learning to write, to write well, to write badly, to write angrily, from learning to despise to learning to abominate, to abominate well, to abominate badly, to abominate abominably, to rant, to fulminate, to shout down the sea, to age, to age gracefully, to age awkwardly, to age at all, to think, to regret, to list himself in the newspapers under "Lost and Found," might culminate precisely in this: a roaring, raging, crazy mad passionate bibliography.

L'Lapse

A SCENARIO FOR MICHELANGELO ANTONIONI

The scene is the plaza in front of the Plaza. Seated near the fountain are Marcello, a wealthy film critic who has enriched himself by writing attacks on Akira Kurosawa for the American Legion Magazine, *and Anna, a lengthy, elegant beauty, blond, whose extreme nervousness is exteriorized in thumb-sucking. Shabby-looking pigeons wheel about meaningfully but in slow motion. The fountain supplies the sound of falling water; the water sounds viscid, hopeless. Anna is a wealthy, bored young animal, rather chunky in the hindquarters—more eland than gazelle. Marcello is a failed poet. If the budget permits, there may be a scene, late in the film, in which Marcello pours lysergic acid all over a rival poet's verses—a nasty business. The pace of the opening is slow; in fact, the entire film will proceed as if the players were wearing lead suits. The camera begins by thoughtfully considering a nearby construction project (played by the Tishman Brothers), fondling with love each girder and bag of cement; then, reluctantly, it tears itself away to focus on Anna. Anna, looking as if her gums are getting sore, examines her thumbs; the right thumb is distinctly larger than the left. She lifts her eyes to regard Marcello—a slow, somnolent, yet intensely meaningful regard, which is held for seven minutes. Finally, she speaks.*

ANNA (*slowly, sadly*): A superb drama. An engrossing film . . . penetratingly different . . . makes cinema history.

MARCELLO (*wealthy, bored*): If I'm going to teach you the business, *cara,* you gotta learn not to make adverbs out of words like "penetrating." Now go on. It's one of the year's ten best, I suppose?

ANNA: One of the year's ten best. Urgent. Sheer cinematic excitement.

MARCELLO: A magnificent, ironic parable?

ANNA: A magnificent ironic parable. Eerily symbolic in intent and effect. Beautiful to watch. (*Inserts thumb*)

MARCELLO: Say something about style.

ANNA: A deft and skillful style full of pictorial chic?

MARCELLO (*moodily*): Not bad.

ANNA (*without hope*): An outstanding film for discriminating moviegoers. Does not merely survive repeated visits, it repays them. Original and remarkable. Intellectual suspense, mystery, and excitement. A film to see. A film worth seeing. A film of disturbing beauty. Marvelously realized. (*Turns face away*) Oh, Marcello, it's no good. I can't do it. Last night . . .

MARCELLO (*sharply, annoyed*): I don't want to talk about last night. Now, what about the director?

ANNA: A sensualist with a camera.

MARCELLO: That's very good. Go on. This is a review in depth.

ANNA: A poet with a camera. A philosopher with a camera. Another damn Italian with a camera.

MARCELLO: Anna!

ANNA (*removes thumb*): But, Marcello, I didn't *like* the picture. I was bored.

MARCELLO: Look, sweets, it doesn't matter you were bored. The point is, you were bored *in a certain way*. Like brilliantly.

ANNA: You didn't think it was a little . . . slow?

MARCELLO: *Of course* it was slow. I mean it had a certain slow beauty. A sort of visual rubato. On the other hand, it was obscure and baffling.

ANNA: Visual rubato?

MARCELLO: I mean you can't just say you were *bored*, for God's sake.

ANNA (*trailing thumb in fountain*): Marcello . . .

MARCELLO (*evasively*): Yes?

ANNA: You know what's wrong . . . between us?

MARCELLO (*more evasively*): What?

ANNA: We have to face it, Marcello. We communicate. You and me.

MARCELLO (*shamed, looks away*): I know . . .

ANNA: We communicate like crazy.

MARCELLO: Anna . . .

ANNA: It's so *déclassé*. I can't bear it. (*Reinserts thumb*)

MARCELLO: It's my fault. I have a tendency to make myself clear. I mean . . .

ANNA (*bitterly*): I *know* what you mean.

(*Shot of sky—overbright, glaring. Overexposed? Shot of cement bag—fat, opulent even, manufacturer's name clearly visible. Shot of boy on bicycle looking over shoulder, away from camera. Shot of puddle of water, Juicy Fruit wrapper floating on surface.*)

MARCELLO: Anna?

ANNA: Last night . . .

MARCELLO: I could change. My approach, I mean. (*Speaks in italics*) *These rooms, these corridors, empty, endless, oppressive; the mirrors on the walls, dark, ancient, oppressive; the carved frames, elaborate ceilings. These rooms, these corridors . . .* Where did you put my pills?

ANNA (*searches in handbag*): I have them—here. I wish you wouldn't.

MARCELLO (*chews pills*): I can't help it. I'm nervous. It's that new picture I have to see tomorrow—the one I've been putting off. *Lawrence or Arabia? Lawrence over Arabia? I* don't know. All I know is, I'm afraid of it.

ANNA: What's to be afraid?

MARCELLO (*dismally*): I hear it's a picture, you know, in the old tradition. Swift-moving, panoramic. With *action.* I'm not sure I'll be able to cope.

ANNA (*brutally*): You're as good as you ever were, Marcello.

(MARCELLO *winces. They regard each other for a long moment. Shot of nail kegs at construction site. Camera peers into keg, counts nails. Shot of bus disappearing around corner. Shot of I.R.T. breaking down. Shot of man in undershirt high on apartment balcony. Shot of little girl with balloon.*)

ANNA: Last night . . .

MARCELLO (*pulls himself together*): Forget about last night. Think about tonight. What's for supper?

ANNA: Steak. The way you like it.

MARCELLO: With peanut butter?

ANNA: Yes.

MARCELLO: God, that's decadent.

ANNA (*pleased, smiles*): Yes.

MARCELLO: Don't you think that's just a little . . . Fellini?

ANNA (*enigmatically*): Yes.

(*Shot of passenger pigeons against bleak sky. Shot of man waiting for bus; bus fails to appear—he is waiting on Park Avenue. Long shot of traffic light changing on Fordham Road. Close shot of unsmoked filter-tip cigarette; it looks virginal, possibly inhibited.*)

ANNA (*removes thumb*): Last night . . .

MARCELLO (*ignores her, reads from magazine*): "A prolonged detailed illustration of the moody surrender of a woman to a rare and elusive love." Crowther, *Times*. How do you like that?

ANNA (*thumb*): I like it. "Moody surrender." It's beautiful.

MARCELLO: It's pure pasta, that's what it is. Listen to this: "Antonioni is so selective and sensitive with his use of camera, so deft in catching intonations of emotional flux and flow in the graphic relations of individuals to the vividly passing scene—" I can't go on.

ANNA (*rare, elusive*): Finish it.

MARCELLO: "—that what might be slow and tedious as a cinematic style actually turns out quite fascinating in his skillful command of it." That's what I call a *really* ugly sentence.

ANNA (*thumb out*): You critics with your jealousies. You disgust me, all of you. *Critic!*

MARCELLO: Anna, I think it's time for your walk.

ANNA: My long, long, aimless walk? Marcello, I don't want to go today.

MARCELLO (*slowly, con amore*): Anna, you must. It's a convention.

ANNA (*thumb*): Will there be meaningless incidents?

MARCELLO (*bored again*): One assumes.

ANNA: A little girl playing with a balloon?

MARCELLO: Undoubtedly.

ANNA: An old man with a terrible lined face reading an Armenian newspaper?

MARCELLO: Wasn't he there yesterday?

ANNA (*despair*): Of course. Of course.

(*Shot of empty street with man lurking in doorway. Is it Orson Welles? No, unfortunately, it is not Orson Welles. Shot of electricity lurking in wall outlet. Shot of hoarding advertising* Sodom and Gomorrah. *Shot of I beams stacked randomly in field. Shot of empty benches in park. Medium shot of tree branches afflicted with Memling's Rot.*)

MARCELLO (*reading picture magazine*): What is this . . . "*surf* board"?

ANNA (*dreamily*): One takes a board—

MARCELLO: Yes?

ANNA: And runs out into the water with it—

MARCELLO: Go on.

ANNA: And sinks.

MARCELLO: Are you sure?

ANNA (*thumb out, gaze fixed on thumb*): Sometimes *two* people take the board and run out into the water with it and sink. Last night—

MARCELLO (*admiringly*): You got a future in the industry, baby. What a gift for empty anecdote!

ANNA: Marcello, *why* do we communicate? Why you and

me? Last night, when we *talked* to each other . . . I couldn't bear it. Why can't we be like other people? Why can't we spend our time in mindless eroticism, like everybody else?

MARCELLO (*hangs head*): I don't know.

ANNA: Last night when we were talking about pure cinema, and I called for a transvaluation of all values, and you said that light was the absence of light—we weren't communicating then, were we? It was just jargon, wasn't it? Just noise?

MARCELLO (*facing the truth*): No, Anna, I'm afraid we *were* communicating. On a rather low level.

ANNA (*frenzied, all thumbs*): I want my life to be *really* meaningless. Like in that film. Such boredom! Such emptiness! Such febrile elegance! It was penetratingly different, a magnificent ironic parable, one of the year's ten best. *Marcello!*

MARCELLO: Meaninglessness like that is not for everybody. Not for you and me, *cara.*

(ANNA *turns away. It is clear that if we could see it her face would reveal an emotion of some kind.* MARCELLO *knows what she is feeling, or appears to. He stretches out his right hand. But he cannot quite reach* ANNA; *she is running off down the street after a disappearing bus.*)

MARCELLO: Anna! (*Slow pause*) Anna?

(*Shot of man on bench looking at camera inquiringly. Shot of cement bags. Shot of leaf floating in gutter; leaf floats down drain. Camera waits four minutes to see if leaf will reappear. It does not reappear. Shot of traffic light; it is stuck. Medium shot of old lady pouring mineral water on head. Close shot of same man on bench; his eyes close.*)

FIN

The Teachings of Don B.:
A Yankee Way of Knowledge

While doing anthropological field work in Manhattan
some years ago I met, on West Eleventh Street, a male
Yankee of indeterminate age whose name, I was told, was
Don B. I found him leaning against a building in a profound torpor—perhaps the profoundest torpor I have
ever seen. He was a tallish man with an unconvincing
beard and was dressed, in the fashion of the Village, in
jeans and a blue work shirt. After we had been introduced, by a mutual acquaintance, I explained to him
that I had been told he knew the secrets of certain hallucinogenic substances peculiar to Yankee culture and in
which I was professionally interested. I expressed a wish
to learn what he knew and asked if I might talk with him

about the subject. He simply stared at me without replying, and then said, "No." However, taking note of the dis-
may which must have been plain on my face, he said that
I might return, if I wished, in two years. In the mean-
time, he would think about my proposal. Then he closed
his eyes again, and I left him.

I returned in the summer of 1968 and found Don B.
still leaning against the same building. His torpor was
now something very close to outright gloom, but he
greeted me civilly enough. Again I asked him if he would
consider taking me under instruction. He stared at me
for a long time and then said, "Yes." But, he warned me,
states of nonordinary reality could not be attained by just
anybody, and if just anybody did, by accident, blunder
into a state of nonordinary reality, the anybody might
bloody well regret it. Yankee culture was a fearsome
thing, he told me, and not to be entered into lightly, but
only with a prepared heart. Was I willing, he asked, to
endure the pain, elation, shock, terror, and boredom of
such an experience? Was I, for example, ticklish? I as-
sured him that I was ready and was not ticklish, or not
overmuch. He then led me into the building against
which he had been leaning. He showed me into a small
but poorly furnished apartment containing hundreds of
books stacked randomly about. In the center of the room
a fire was blazing brightly. Throwing a few more books
on the fire, Don B. invited me to be seated, and we had
the first of what proved to be a long series of conversations. The following material, reproduced from my field
notes, has been edited somewhat to eliminate the dull
parts, but in the main reflects accurately what took place
during the period when I was Don B.'s apprentice.

In dealing with any system of world interpretation different from our own, it is necessary to make use of the technique of suspended judgment. This I have done, and I urge the reader to do so also.

June 11, 1968

We were sitting cross-legged on the floor of Don B.'s apartment, facing each other, with the fire, which was kept going even in summer, between us. I decided to ask Don B. about the fire, for it was markedly hot in the room.

"Why is the fire burning, Don B.? It's hot in here."

Don B. gazed at me for a time without answering. Then he said: "Fire burns because it is his nature to burn. Fire is a friend. But one must know how to treat him. He contains a thousand invisible *brillos* which, unleashed, can cause considerable harm to life and property. That is why we have fire engines. The fire engines throw water on Fire and drown the invisible *brillos*. They fear water."

"What is a *brillo*, Don B.?"

"A sort of devil who is invisible."

"But why doesn't your fire burn a hole in the floor?"

"Because I understand Fire and know his secrets," Don B. said. "When I was a boy in the city of Philadelphia, Fire seized many houses, shops, and other buildings and burned them to the ground. But he never seized my house because I knew his secrets and he knew I knew his secrets. Therefore he stayed away."

"What *are* his secrets, Don B.?"

Don B. laughed uproariously.

"You are a fool," he said. "You are not a man of knowledge. Only a man of knowledge can understand secrets.

Even if I told you Fire's secrets, they would be of no use to you."

"Can I become a man of knowledge, Don B.?"

Don B. fell silent. He stared at his knees for some moments. Then he gave me an intense look.

"Maybe," he said.

I went away filled with a powerful and deep sense of warmth.

June 13, 1968

We were sitting as before on the floor of Don B.'s apartment.

"What is a man of knowledge, Don B.?" I asked him.

"A man of knowledge," Don B. replied, "is one who knows. He not only knows, he knows that he knows. He has an ally to help him know."

"What does the ally do, Don B.?"

"The ally helps the man of knowledge know and also helps him know that he knows."

"Do you have an ally, Don B.?"

"Of course."

"Who is your ally, Don B.?"

"Turkey," he said, and laughed uproariously.

I went away filled with a sensation of not having heard him correctly.

June 17, 1968

I had brought Don B. some food. We sat on the floor eating fettucine on rye in silence. I had noticed that although Don B. as a rule ate very little, whenever there were two sandwiches on the floor he ate both halves of his and half of mine, which I thought a little strange.

Without warning he said: "You feel uncomfortable."

I admitted that I felt a bit uncomfortable.

"I knew that you felt uncomfortable," he said. "That is because you have not found your spot. Move around the room until you have found it."

"How do you mean, move around the room?"

"I mean, like sit in different places."

Don B. rose and left the apartment. I tried sitting in different places. What he had said made no sense to me. True, I had been slightly uncomfortable in the spot I had been sitting in. But no other place in the room seemed any better to me. I sat experimentally in various areas but could discover no spot that felt any better than any other spot. I was sweating and felt more uncomfortable than ever. An hour passed, then two hours. I was sitting as hard as I could, first in one place, then another. But no particular place seemed desirable or special. I wondered where Don B. was. Then I noticed that a particular spot near the south wall was exuding a sort of yellow luminosity. I painfully sat over toward it, sit by sit, a process which consumed some twelve minutes. Yes! It was true. In the spot occupied by the yellow luminosity I felt much more comfortable than I had felt in my original spot. The door opened and Don B. entered, smiling.

"Where have you been, Don B.?"

"I caught a flick. I see that you have found your spot."

"You were right, Don B. This spot is much better than my old spot."

"Of course. You were sitting too close to the fire, idiot."

"But Don B.! What is this yellow luminosity that seems to hover over this particular spot?"

"It's the lamp, dummy."

I looked up. Don B. was right. Immediately above my new spot was a light fixture containing two 150-watt bulbs. It was turned on.

I went away filled with a powerful sensation having to do with electricity.

Once again I had asked Don B. about the famous hallucinogenic substances used by the Yankees.

Without replying, he carefully placed another book on the fire. It was Elias Ashmole's *Theatrum chemicum Britannicum.*

"When I sneeze, the earth shakes," Don B. said, after a time.

I greeted this announcement with a certain amount of skepticism.

"Show me, Don B.," I said.

"The man of knowledge does not sneeze on command," he said. "He sneezes only when it is appropriate and right to do so, that is, when his *brillo* is inside his nose, tickling him."

"When is it appropriate and right to sneeze, Don B.?"

"It is appropriate and right to sneeze when your *brillo* is inside your nose, tickling it."

"Does each man have his own personal *brillo,* Don B.?"

"The man of knowledge both *has* a *brillo* and *is* a *brillo.* That is why he is able to sneeze so powerfully that when he sneezes, the earth shakes. *Brillo* is nose, arms, legs, liver—the whole shebang."

"But you said a *brillo* was a devil, Don B."

"Some people *like* devils."

"How does the man of knowledge find his personal *brillo*, Don B.?"

"Through the use of certain hallucinogenic substances peculiar to Yankee culture," Don B. said.

"Can I try them?"

Don B. gazed at me for a long time—an intense gaze. Then he said: "Maybe."

I departed with a strong sense of epistemological obfuscation.

June 20, 1968

"The four natural enemies of the man of knowledge," Don B. said to me, "are fear, sleep, sex, and the Internal Revenue Service."

I listened attentively.

"Before one can become a man of knowledge one must conquer all of these."

"Have you conquered the four natural enemies of the man of knowledge, Don B.?"

"All but the last," he said with a grimace. "Those sumbitches never give up."

"How does one conquer fear, Don B.?"

"One takes a frog and sews it to one's shoe," he said.

"The right or the left?"

Don B. gave me a pitying look.

"Well you'd look mighty funny going down the street with only one frog sewed to your shoes, wouldn't you?" he said. "One frog on *each* shoe."

"How does having frogs sewed to your shoes help one conquer fear, Don B.?"

But Don B. had fallen asleep. I was torn inside. My most deeply held values, such as being kind to frogs, had been placed in question. I really did want to become a man of knowledge. But at such a cost?

June 21, 1968

Today Don B. looked at me for a long time. His gaze, usually so piercing, was suffused with a sort of wet irony.

"Xavier," he said, "there is something about you I like. I think it's your credulity. Belief is very important if one wishes to become a man of knowledge—to truly 'see.' I think you might possibly be able to 'see' someday. But 'seeing' is very difficult. Only after the most arduous preparation of the heart will you be able to 'see.' Even though you are not a Yankee, it may be that you will be able to prepare your heart adequately. I don't know. I'm not guaranteeing anything."

"How does one prepare the heart, Don B.?"

"One cleanses it with either a yellow warmth or a pink luminosity. I don't know which is right in your case. It varies with the individual. Each man must choose. So we will try both. But I must warn you that the experience is dangerous and sticky. Your life may hang on how you behave in the next hour. You must do everything exactly as I tell you. This isn't kid stuff, buddy."

I was filled with a sense of awe and dread. Could I, a Western man, enter into the darkest mysteries of the Yankees without putting myself and my most deeply held convictions in peril? A profound sadness overtook me, followed by an indescribable anguish. I suppressed them.

"All right, Don B.," I said. "If you really think I'm ready."

Don B. then rose and went to a cupboard. He opened it and removed two vessels which he placed on the floor, near the fire. He opened a second cupboard and pro-

duced two ordinary drinking glasses, which he also
placed on the floor. Then he went into another room, re-
turning with a sort of crock with a lid on it, a small round
yellow object, and a knife. All of these he placed on the
floor near the fire. He knelt alongside them and began a
strange, rather eerie chant. I could not make out all of
the words but they included "town," "pony," and
"feather." I wondered if I was supposed to chant too, but
dared not interrupt him to ask. I began chanting, tenta-
tively, "town-pony-feather."

Abruptly, Don B. stopped chanting and began whit-
tling at the small yellow object. Was it this, I wondered,
that generated the "yellow warmth" he had spoken of?
Soon there was a small pile of yellow-white chips before
him. He then reached for one of the vessels he had taken
from the cupboard and poured a colorless liquid, perhaps four ounces of it, into each of the drinking glasses.
Then he crossed his eyes and sat with his eyes crossed for
some moments. I crossed my eyes also. We sat thus for
four minutes, our gazes missing each other but meeting, I felt, somewhere in the neutral space on either side
of us. The sensation was strange, eerie.

Don B. uncrossed his eyes, blinked, smiled at me.

He reached for the second vessel and poured a second
colorless liquid into each glass, but much less of it: about
half an ounce per glass, I estimated. He then removed
the top of the crock and took from it six small colorless
objects, each perhaps an inch and one-half square, plac-
ing three of them in each glass. Next he picked up one of
the yellow-white chips and rubbed it around the rim of
each glass. Then he stirred the mixtures with his index
finger and handed me a glass.

"Drink it down without stopping," he said, "for if you

pause in the drinking of it the *brillo* which it summons, your personal *brillo,* will not appear. And the whole thing will be a bloody goddamn fiasco."

I did as Don B. bade me, and drained the glass in one gulp. Immediately a horrible trembling convulsed my limbs, while an overwhelming nausea retracted my brain. I flopped around on the floor a lot. I became aware of (left to right) a profound sadness, a yellow warmth, an indescribable anguish, and a pink luminosity. Don B. was watching me with a scornful smile on his face. I was sweating, my stomach was cramping, and I needed a cigarette. I saw, on my left, the profound sadness merging with the yellow warmth, and on my right, the indescribable anguish intermingling with the pink luminosity, and, suddenly, standing with one foot on the profound sadness/yellow warmth and the other on the indescribable anguish/pink luminosity, a gigantic figure half-human, half-animal, and a hundred feet tall (roughly). A truly monstrous thing! Never in the wildest fantasies of fiction had I encountered anything like it. I looked at it in complete, utter bewilderment. It was strange and eerie, and yet familiar. Then I realized with a shock of horror, terror, and eeriness that it was a colossal Publisher, and that it was moving toward me, wanted something from me. I fainted. When I revived, it took me to lunch at Lutèce and we settled on an advance in the low fifties, which I accepted even though I knew I was not yet, in the truest sense, a man of knowledge. But there would be other books, I reflected, to become a man of knowledge in, and if I got stuck I could always go back and see good old Don B.

Two

Swallowing

The American people have swallowed a lot in the last four years. A lot of swallowing has been done. We have swallowed electric bugs, laundered money, quite a handsome amount of grain moving about in mysterious ways, a war more shameful than can be imagined, much else. There are even people who believe that the President does not invariably tell us the truth about himself or ourselves—he tells us *something*, we swallow that.

In the history of swallowing, the disposition of the enormous cheese—six feet thick, twenty feet in diameter, four thousand pounds—which had been Wisconsin's principal contribution to the New York World's Fair of 1964–5, is perhaps instructive.

The problem was that Wisconsin, the fair being over and all that, did not want the cheese back. Jurisdictional haggle between the state of New York, host state as it were to the enormous *fromage,* and the state of Wisconsin, the gorgeous gouda's owner of record, was carried on over a period of months.

The then-governor of the Dairy State wrote officially to the governor of the Empire State, suggesting that the cheese be thought of as a gift from the people of the Dairy State to the people of the Empire State. The latter could, for example, eat it, he said. The governor of the Empire State replied courteously that although he, the elected *jefe grande* and representative in all matters of the people of the Empire State, was deeply sensible of the honor being extended to the people of his state by their well-loved fellow citizens in Wisconsin, there just wasn't a whole bunch of interest in this-here six-foot-thick, twenty-foot-in-diameter, four-thousand-pound cheese among the insensitive civilians who made up the raw material of his (the guv's) suzerainty, and could the state of Wisconsin have it off the premises by Thursday.

The governor of the Dairy State then wondered, by registered letter, if the governor of the Empire State might not in some sense be offering insult and hurt to the people of his own (Dairy) State by rejecting this beautiful gift which was, all authorities agreed, not less than top-hole in its line, that is to say, cheeseness.

The governor of the Empire State then hinted tele-graphically that the motives of the governor of the Dairy State might be something less than unimpugnable, might in fact have something to do with certain expenses incur-rable by removal of said artifact to turf of origin, and fur-

ther toyed (telegraphically) with the possibility that
cheeseparing in the pejorativist of senses might be a way
of life in Madison, Milwaukee, and Eau Claire.

The governor of the Dairy State countered in a bull
covered with seals and ribbons and delivered by a masked
motorcycle messenger once in the employ of the late Jean
Cocteau that since it was well-known that his dear friend
and fellow practitioner of the governor hustle presided
over what the World Health Organization had demon-
strated to be the densest rat population per square mile
in America, perhaps the cheese might be utilized for the
nourishment and basic rat needs of this important part of
his esteemed colleague's constituency, and speculated further that the renaming of the Empire State to something
on the order of the Rat State might not be such a bad
idea either.

The governor of the Empire State riposted by fast gun-
boat complete with captain's gig with gold trim and naval
officer with dress sword, white hat under left arm, curly
hair, deep blue (piercing; steady) eyes that the governor
of the Curd State, as he (the governor of the Emp. State)
liked to think of it . . .

From there the dialogue degenerated. The cheese
meanwhile was developing a certain fetor.

The problem was solved in the following way. The
cheese was presented as a gift free of charge and for
nothing and with no strings attached to a young poet.
The poet, starving as all poets are ordained to be in their
beardless poetpuppyhood, had been subsisting on a daily
input of one (1) pot of warm water over which one (1)
chicken bone had been waved, once. He immediately
boogied out to the former fairgrounds and took up resi-

dence in, around, amid, etc., the six-foot-thick, twenty-foot-in-diameter, four-thousand-pound cheese. It sustained him for two years and three days. He prospered and grew fat and his art prospered and grew fat also. He wrote verse melic and gnomic, odes and epodes, dithyrambs and dirges, hymns, chanties, lays, epithalamia, and things to be chiseled on tombstones in fine-flowing Caslon letters than which no letters are more comely. He lives among us still and there is no tree from which a bird cannot be charmed by the sweet soft steel of his verse. His best-known line, one that will undoubtedly sing forever in the hearts of men and possibly their heads also, refers directly back to his experience of the cheese: *"I can't believe I ate the whole thing."*

The American people have swallowed quite a lot in the last four years, but as the poet cited goes on to say, there are remedies.

1972

The Young Visitirs

Basker and Letitia Filter had been in Washington only two days when a fairly good friend invited them to the White House for a party to be hosted by the President himself.

"Basker," Letitia said, "maybe this will be too fine a party for us plain folks from the South. They will just look at us and know that we are plain and from the South and not high and mighty."

"Stuff," Basker replied. "We are as good as anybody and fairly mighty, too, since I made my fortune in the Persian Gulf, and, besides, I voted for him."

"But do not wear the green hat," Letitia said. "It clashes and makes you look as if from the South."

"This is the finest hat in all of Oklahoma," Basker said. "And, besides, I have stuck some poems in it by Walt Whitman, the poet of Health, Education, and Welfare, that I plan to read to the Chief Executive if I get a chance."

The first person they saw when they arrived was their friend Code d'Havenon, who was a well-known intimate of the President and had fixed them up with the invitation. Code was wearing glittering court dress, accompanied by an appropriately plummy manner, which contrasted sharply with Basker's and Letitia's air of social unease. "Well, there!" Code exclaimed. "It's old Basker and Letitia! How are you chaps tonight? Basker, take off that green hat. Letitia, you are as heartwarming as ever!" He bent and kissed her hands as they walked through the long lines of silent gendarmes toward the fun.

Then, the famous East Room, where a sparkling throng was displaying a lot of flash. The electricity was being wasted with a lavish hand, and there were three string bands in strange uniforms. Code d'Havenon took Basker and Letitia around, introducing them to the top levels of American productivity.

"But where is the President?" Basker asked. "I don't see him. Is he here?"

"He is upstairs in his study, working on the nation," Code said suavely. "Usually, he doesn't come down until eleven o'clock, to tell us that it's time to go to bed. He is the father of us all, and that is heavy work, believe me. And now I must leave you, because I spy over there the head of the World Loan Office and I have to speak to him for a moment about a matter. Have a good time and try not to be too gauche."

"That Code has got a little stuck up since he's been up

here in Washington, you know that?" Basker said to Letitia.

She was grazing among the stumpy bottles of the drinks table, looking for some grass. "Well, he *is* a famous P.R. man, well-known for his fabulous entrée into the regime," she replied, "so I expect that's the way they act and he's just doing what he must. Don't be so hard on people, Basker. You're not perfect, either, you know."

Then, magically, the President was in the room, flanked by tackles, guards, and ends, and backed by three very big linebackers. "Peace, my children!" he said, and then everyone got up from a kneeling position and resumed their conversations, sort of, but turned now toward the sun of his high visibility.

"You reckon I ought to ask him what I want to ask him now?" Basker said worriedly. "Or wait?"

"Well, Godamighty, Basker, I've never known you to be bashful before," Letitia said. "And, besides, you are an influential citizen on your home ground."

"But he never answered my letters."

The President was bent over a lady, smiling and holding on to her fingernails.

"Citizen President," Basker said, "my name is Basker Filter? And I'm from Norman, Oklahoma? And I just wondered if you had a minute? 'Cause there's some things I been wantin' to speak to you about?"

The guards and tackles and linebackers moved in on Basker very fast, but the President stayed them with a hand.

"Pleased to meet you, Mr. Filter," the President said. "I'm always pleased to speak to any of my children—even the bad ones. What's on your mind?"

"Well," Basker said, "the folks back in Norman—and,

indeed, the whole state—are gettin' kinda upset about the teeter-totter. The giant teeter-totter you're buildin' for us that's gonna reach from Maine to California?"

"Are you referring to the U.S. Interstate Bicentennial Teeter-Totter?"

"That's the one," Basker said. "I know we don't know anything about anything, being from the South and all, but a bunch of people down home are still hongry. And this here teeter-totter is costin' just a sight of money, and half the schoolhouses in Norman don't have no chalk, and some folks in Norman are *eatin'* chalk, and—"

"Those individuals are certainly welcome to stay in any country that welcomes them," the President said. "We all make mistakes, and in my view eating chalk is a mistake. But we have to pay for our mistakes. That is a rule of life. They certainly can't expect to ride on the Teeter-Totter. Teeter-tottering is good for you and it has important moral/economic ramifications that you don't understand, being underage, morally/economically speaking. But let me give you something to take back to Norman with you. Ralph?"

One of the linebackers offered the President a brown paper bag. The President stuck his hand in and pulled out a large, red, round lollipop. "Here you are, Mr. Filter. Enjoy yourself. With my blessings and good wishes."

"Mr. President, this here is a poem by Walt Whitman," Basker said. "It makes what I feel is a very important statement?"

The President looked puzzled. Then he reached into the bag again and pulled out another lollipop. "Here you are, Mr. Filter. Enjoy yourself. With my blessings and good wishes." And he moved away.

The Palace

I was standing in line at the bank (Chase Manhattan Fourteenth Street) last Friday, and I happened to notice the amount of the check the short Puerto Rican woman in front of me was cashing: $84.06. I looked away very quickly, but the check was yellow and I noticed that there were a lot of white and black and Puerto Rican women in line holding in their hands the same yellow paycheck. And I thought, $84.06, that's not much for a week's work. Then I tried to remember what the federal minimum wage was, and remembered, and tried to multiply $1.60 by forty hours and got it wrong, and more women were coming into the bank now with these yellow checks

in their hands (it was lunchtime), and I began running down the purchasing power of $84.06. It's a single session with a $50-an-hour analyst, with $34.06 left over for coffee, cakes, and the rent. And a lady I know has informed me that her pantyhose cost $2.50 the pair, and a kennel owner I know has offered me a purebred Rhodesian Ridgeback for $350, and you can buy a Pontiac Firebird for $4,385. And a house in the country . . .

But you can get a pretty good tennis racquet for $84.06, and all of a sudden I flashed on a scene in which all these ladies, white, black, and Puerto Rican, were zipping into Abercrombie's or somewhere and lashing out their $84.06's for brand-new tennis racquets. And for a minute, there in the bank line, every yellow check became in my mind a good-quality tennis racquet, all these ladies were waving good-quality tennis racquets, and what else was there to do with these tennis racquets but *beat me to death with them?* What if the Revolution occurred to all these women simultaneously? What if they put it together, figured it out, got hold of the real numbers, all at once, and then, armed with their death-dealing Bancrofts or Wilsons, and me armed only with a little card that says I'm a member of the A.C.L.U., came after me? Because my check wasn't yellow and it wasn't for $84.06, and although I am for the Revolution in principle I haven't done much about it lately in a practical way. So in order not to think about this distressing situation I thought about the palace.

The palace is quite a wonderful place, full of Eames chairs and Barcelona chairs and Pollock paintings and David Smith sculptures and other high-class cultural grid coordinates. The palace was partly designed by Breuer,

but then Mies came over one day while the thing was still
a-building and said something about how wouldn't it be
nice if the travertine that covers the west wall ran *this* way
instead of *that* way (waving his hands in the air, which is
how architects do their thinking), and Breuer, who is the
most modest of men, said, "Mies, just for fun, why don't
you do part of it and *I'll* do part of it and we'll see what
happens." Well, Mies liked to play, too, so he agreed, and
then when Corbu visited the site *he* wanted to get in on it,
and, in fact, the entire east wing is Corbu's. And then
Nervi and Aalto and Neutra and Saarinen and Louis
Kahn and all sorts of other people, all geniuses, got interested, contributed bits, ideas, little pieces, because none
of them had ever done a palace before—I mean a real,
honest-to-God palace, as opposed to a corporate head-
quarters. The king came out to the site every day wearing
a blue hardhat and was just beside himself. I have never
seen a king, even a limited constitutional monarch, take
so much pleasure in anything. The wonderful part was
that the whole place *worked*, it came together beautifully,
none of the architects tried to upstage each other—the
palace appears to be the product of a single hand. Kahn's
dark-red brick towers look amazing and lovely against
Mies's exposed steel (in this case, Cor-Ten, which rusts to
a handsome reddish brown, rather than his usual black-
painted steel—just one instance of the courtesy and tact
and sweetness that prevailed). Aalto used dark woods instead of light, Le Corbusier did not insist on pilotis, and
everyone wondered what Wright would have done if he
had been around to participate, and Venturi jumped up
and down and clapped his hands in glee and sent a tele-
gram to Paolo Soleri, out there in the desert, and ordered

forty dozen wind bells and wondered if Soleri would be interested in doing the grand ballroom. Soleri was enchanted with the idea of doing a grand ballroom, and the next day the model arrived by air express, together with a blueprint forty feet long and so splendid in conception that everybody agreed it gave new meaning to the words "grand" and "ballroom." And the throne room, done by Simon Rodia, who did the Watts Towers, is as gaudy as Gaudí, and the royal kitchens, by Edward Durell Stone, make you want to get in there and cook your heart out.

The royal tennis courts extend for miles in every direction—grass courts set in glades and dells (each glade and dell the work of a great-grandson of Frederick Law Olmsted himself), and I suddenly shouted, right out loud, there in line at Chase Manhattan Fourteenth Street, "Tennis, everyone?" And everyone shouted back, "Yes, yes, *tennis!*" And we all set out, the white and black and Puerto Rican women with their tennis racquets, and the clerks and tellers, too, with their racquets, and even the bank officers, in their dark suits, with their racquets, in a long straggle, or friendly mob, in the direction of the palace. The palace exists; we have only to get there—that is, walk hard enough. That is a beautiful idea of which I have always been very fond. The truth is that the palace does not exist but the serfs do.

The Dragon

One day a wan and scruffy dragon came to the city looking for a disease. He had in mind ending his life, which he felt to be tedious, unsatisfactory, tax-troubled, lacking in purpose. Looking up diseases in the Yellow Pages, and finding none, he decided to enroll himself in a hospital. At St. Valentine's, he approached a guard and asked the way to the No Hope Ward. Directed to the proper floor, he found there a bed newly made, white-washed with sheets. He climbed in and turned on the television set, which was attached to the bed umbilically. A nurse motored in.

"What have you got?" asked the dragon, thinking of diseases.

"Everything," said the nurse. "Eclampsia to milk leg. There is nothing that we do not have. Our Intensive Despair Unit is the envy of the profession. You will be edified. Everything will be all right. Trust us. The world is waiting for the sunrise."

The subsequent examinations, consultations, testifications can easily be imagined. To the point. The hospital refused to give him a disease. After three days, he'd been offered not so much as a nip of pneumonia.

"I trusted you," he said to his nurse. His fine fiery eyes regarded her with reproach and disgust.

"I thought for a while we had something worked out with the Kidney Committee," she said. "But when they discovered the precise nature of your undertaking . . ."

Thinking of diseases still, the dragon left the hospital. Many fine diseases passed through his mind—rabies, gout, malaria, rinderpest. Or, he thought suddenly, I could get myself slain by a hero.

At that moment, a Colonel of Sanitation came striding by, in his green uniform. "You there!" he cried. "Ho, dragon, stop and patter for a bit. Quickly, quickly— haven't got all day! There are Mr. Goodbar wrappers in the streets still, after all my efforts, and the efforts of my men, day in day out—people, people, if we could just do something about the people, then perhaps an end to the endlessness. One could go home of a Friday night, and wipe the brow, and doff the uniform, and thank God for a day well squandered. But you—you have a strange aspect. What kind of a thing are you? Are you disposable? Biodegradable? Ordinary citizen out for a stroll? Looking for work? Member of a conspiracy? Vegetable? Mineral? Two-valued? Hostile to the national interest of the Department of Sanitation? Thrill-crazed kid? Objet d'art? Circus in town?"

"I am nothing much," said the dragon. "But I must declare, if you will allow me, that I am in a catatony of admiration *in re* your life task. Your labor is indeed Sisyphean."

"You look rather like one of our fine Department of Sanitation trucks," said the colonel, "now that I regard you closely. Are you sure you are not a malingering Sanitation truck?"

"I don't think so," said the dragon.

"Let it go," the colonel said, with a sigh. "Let it go, like so much else in this radically imperfect world, in this radically befilthed city. This is my lunch hour, after all. Would you care to rip up a chop? I like your style, know a place—quiet talk, exchange of views, not-bad Gibsons, pretty waitresses, Diners Club and American Express cards accepted."

They sat over their tasty and well-onioned Gibsons.

"Tell me," said the dragon. "Are you West Point?"

"Sandhurst," said the colonel. "Now, what is it, exactly, that is eating you and making you wan? Some order of death wish, I would imagine."

"That is the case," said the dragon, "exactly."

"A question of existence," said the colonel, "or its opposite."

"You have put your finger on it," said the dragon.

"Dragons exist," said the colonel. "Only a fool would doubt it."

"If pricked, do I not bleed?"

"You suffer, however, from a sort of general meaninglessness."

"Since the thirteenth century."

The colonel thought for a moment. "You could be an endangered species," he said. "That would give you a meaningful life role. We love and cherish our endangered species and extend to them every courtesy."

"Well . . ."

"By the authority vested in me by the Department of Sanitation," pronounced the colonel, "I hereby declare you an endangered species, *in tenebris, inter alia, pro forma, primus inter pares,* and subject to approval at the highest levels."

"Thank you," said the dragon. "Thank you very much."

"The President himself is vitally interested in endangered species," said the colonel. "He has a list."

"Are men on it?"

The colonel rose up in a great fit of anger and threw his glass into the fire. Half a Gibson followed it into the flames. He then stamped from the room with skillful majesty, excellent hauteur, and the bill. The dragon, filled with self-regard and convinced that he had at last gotten a message to the Authorities, bought a two-dollar lottery ticket and decided to stop smoking.

An Hesitation on the Bank of the Delaware

"Well, General Washington, sir, we are just about ready to croff the Delaware. The men are ready. Their morale is good. The boats are prepared. Shall I give the word?"

"Just a moment, Major Kinsolving. A dispatch rider is due, carrying word of the ftate of the heating plant in my houfe in Virginia. It's been acting awfully cranky. And another dispatch rider is due, bringing news of the well that is being dug at my estate at Fig Island, off the Carolinas. We have gone down forty-three feet and not yet got water. And I await ftill another messenger, carrying intelligence of my summer home in Georgia. We've been having a few problems with the fenestration. Rude boys have been breaking windows by throwing giant crayfish at them. It's moft annoying."

"But, General, unless we launch the boats pretty shortly, the attack will lose the element of furprife. Dawn is faft approaching. Although I admit nobody likes to have his carpets littered with wet, muddy giant crayfish."

"And then there is the matter of the mosquito nets for my tiny little retreat and hideaway in the Louisiana territory. The mosquitoes down there are fomething fierce, Kinsolving."

"You certainly have a lot of houfes, General. Although I'm not being critical. I understand. Everybody understands. The four million pounds that these houfes have coft the infant Republic doesn't bother us a bit. Even though most of us have had to sell our cow to pay for them. We didn't need a cow anyway. A cow was, for most of us, an unnecessary luxury. The fecurity of your mind and person is, of courfe, paramount."

"You do understand, Kinsolving. You showed that when you picked out the wallpaper for my houfe in Angle, Vermont. That was nice wallpaper."

"No more than you deserve, General, you being the Father of Our Country and all. No man can lead the patriots into battle without solid-silver wallpaper in his houfe. Or one of his houfes. The General Fervices Administration howled, of courfe."

"Is the General Fervices Administration standing on the bank of this river, preparing to launch one of the decifive battles of the war? No. No, it is not. But to business. My boat. Is the hand-carved rosewood seat in place?"

"It is, General. The Fecret Fervice installed it. Although I might point out that you're fuppofed to be ftanding up. Wrapped in your cloak against the icy winds. A ftern and determined expression on your vifage."

"A good bunch of boys, the Fecret Fervice. What about the beaten-gold boat bottom?"

"Done and done. The gold-beaters have finished their arduous labor."

"Are the costly Oriental rugf in place, on the farther shore?"

"Yef."

"And the golf courfe?"

"Eighteen holes, General, each hole and approach beautifully landscaped by private contributions extracted from a grateful and nearly beggared citizenry. You have a fourfome scheduled with Cornwallis and the other soon-to-be-defeated Limey generals at three-thirty fharp."

"Very good, Kinsolving. To the boats, then. But wait! I just remembered. What about the houfe for my horfe? Have the funds been appropriated?"

"Sir, I regret to tell you that there can be no houfe for your horfe. Both the Houfe Appropriations Committee and the Horfe Appropriations Committee bounced it back."

"No houfe for my horfe?"

"The Continental Congress resolved that your famous plainneff and modefty would be ill ferved were it known that a houfe for your horfe was paid for from the public purfe."

"No houfe for my poor horfe! Oh, vile! My horfe, houfeless! Suddenly I feel infecure, Kinsolving—terribly,

terribly infecure. Tell the army to get out of the boats. And send the Congress a ftatement: One river crossing under hazardous conditions, two thousand pounds, payable in advance. We don't budge until we get the fhillings."

"Two thousand pounds! The exact cost of the houfe for your horfe!"

"I trust the gentlemen in Philadelphia will get the meffage. If the young nation is to endure, the serenity of my head is crucial, Kinsolving, absolutely crucial. And it takes a heap of houfing to make a head at home."

The Royal Treatment

Written under the pseudonym Lily McNeil

(With apologies to the late Ogden Nash)

I would like to publicly proclaim that I, for one, do not
think the President is guilty of base, low, or tiny-minded
malfeasance

And that although the former Vice-President has made
me sad, at least he didn't do anything that could correctly
be described as high treasance.

And that although the former Attorney General and the
former Secretary of Commerce may or may not be legally
indictable

I think any small petty wrongs they may have committed
are probably readily rightable.

And the former Counsel to the President and the two

former Assistants to the President and the two former
Special Assistants to the President and the former Acting
Director of the F.B.I. are all okay guys in my book, and I
devoutly wish that someone like Little Joe Cartwright,
Spider Man, Alain Robbe-Grillet or the Maharishi could
jump in there and get them off the hook.

And I don't really believe in my heart of hearts that the
President would go so far as to bug his brother,
And the two missing tapes aren't important because since
they didn't exist in the first place how could they contain
any terrible news that somebody might want to suppress,
sequester, stifle, or smother?
And what happened to those admirable gentlemen,
Richardson, Ruckelshaus, and Cox,
Shocked and dismayed me but I was able to drain it from
the wading pool of my mind by reading fourteen improv-
ing tracts by Increase Mather while simultaneously listen-
ing to the complete works of the entire family of Bachs.
Still, all of the accusations and denials and leaks and
plumbing and frocking and unfrocking and hundred-
dollar bills running around in suitcases with no human
hands attached to them except maybe people in red wigs
and furor and shouting and high-level pomposity
Does tend to create in us of the silent majority a degree
of what might be called anonymosity.

I get the distinct impression that the American form of
government is exhausted and puffing and panting
And that something neater, along the lines of, say, abso-
lute monarchy might be more enchanting.
And so for king I would like to nominate with all due
modesty, me—

The first woman king, to whom in these times of raised consciousness and equal-opportunity employment no fair-minded former voter could object, could he?
People are tired of going into those little booths and looking at those long lists of candidates most of whom they don't even recognize the names of
Wouldn't it be simpler just to have a sovereign that they could cluster in a square when she appeared bowing on a balcony and throw their hats in the air and shout the acclaims of?

We'd save trillions and trillions by abolishing the executive, judicial, and legislative branches with all their offices, buildings, secretaries, pension plans, and places they have to hurry at lunchtime in their official limousines to be at.
Instead, there'd just be me and my fiat.
I don't think we really need all those checks and balances the Constitution provides which leave the czar, caliph, shah, or doge trembling and tense in the air like a Flying Wallenda
A situation in which, you'll admit, it's very difficult to get the people's business justly and efficiently off your callenda.
I promise I wouldn't be lofty, remote, or otherwise unduly regal
I promise I would try to do things in ways that were (definitively, you understand) legal.

And all of the Congress would have to go out and get added to the labor force and seek gainful employment and social utility
Instead of drowning the great issues of the day in a bog

of blather, hebetude, cod's-wallop, and piggy ignobil-
ity.
And all of the Supreme Court justices would have to take
off their robes and put on ordinary suits and ties and go
down and sit in the agora
In obedience to the divine dictum of the hero-architect
Mies van der Rohe that less is mora.
And I wouldn't have anybody near the throne capable of
embarrassing me by his Quasimodic behavior except
maybe my consort, who would probably be Albert, Philip,
Ralph, Igor, or some other name that I love
Which wouldn't prevent me from, if he got out of line,
slapping him upside the head with my velvet hand in its
iron glove.

Lily the First is a nomenclature that I wouldn't mind
responding to, graciously
And I've already spoken to the Moran Company about
the royal barge, spaciously
My proposal is, I admit, anti-democratic, un-American,
and anachronistic
But wouldn't it be better than the present megillah in
which the sacred Persons of the governmental Trinity
find themselves facing each other in postures positively
pugilistic?
And if I did something clearly reprehensible you
wouldn't have to convene eighteen different investigatory
bodies to figure out who to guillotine
There'd only be me, walking in a stately manner in my
best Halston toward the shredding machine.

Mr. Foolfarm's Journal

Mr. Foolfarm, the well-known Generalist, was not in again today. He has hauled Himself to Washington on the Shuttle, to see to his Ambassadorship. The post, as Plenipotentiary to North Minerva (the handsome and vivacious South Pacific atoll) was awarded him not in Consequence of his campaign contribution of $1.95, as malicious Tongues have whispered, but rather for his lifetime of service to the Nation, as well as his great talents at Stroking and Mental Reservation. He is also known to excel at Face-Slapping, holding the world Title for same at 34 hours 20 minutes (Kiev, U.S.S.R., 1961).

•

Mr. Foolfarm was not in again today. He is in Washington, the Capital of the Country, advising an Important Person about Hangout. It had been suggested to the Important Person that he Let It All Hang Out, but Mr. Foolfarm is not entirely Sanguine as to the Consequences of this Policy. The noted Generalist has, it is said, offered a Bouquet of Options including Partial Hangout, Semi-Partial Hangout, Semi-Partial Reversible Hangout, More or Less Total Hangout, and Absolutely Final Weighted Plus-or-Minus Hangout. The Important Person is giving these Choices the consideration they Deserve.

•

Mr. Foolfarm, the Omnidirectional Thinker, was not in again today. He is in Washington, the Capital of the Country, learning to play Tennis. By fierce perusal of the Newspapers, he has learned that if he is ever put away in one of the better government Nicks, he will have to be Able to at least get the Ball back over the net, or else suffer social Obloquy. Golf he has already mastered.

•

It was noticed that the lights burned late at Mr. Foolfarm's house last evening, and again today he is not in it. Reliable information has it that he is in Washington, the Seat of Government, advising the Revenue Service as to What Must Be Done. They are said to be furiously grateful. The celebrated Glossarist is urging that a Pie Chart be added to the first page of the Form, so that the joyous Ratepayer will be enabled to indicate *pristinae virtutis memores* how he wants his Mopus dissipated. Thus if the citizen wishes to pay less for War, for example, he will be able to skimp the War slice of the pie appropriately; and if he wishes to obtain more Booze, he will be able to

sweeten the Booze slice. Mr. Foolfarm has Provided (lest
he be thought a glistering Ninny) that not more than 12
percent of the people's wishes thus expressed be heeded.
The remaining 78 percent of the decision-making process
is to be reserved to the Same Old Crowd. The Crowd has
proposed Mr. Foolfarm for the National Medal and a
bank charter.

•

Mr. Foolfarm, the esteemed Longhead, fled his digs in
Velvet Street at near-midnight last evening, so as not to
be at home again today. He is in Washington, the Country's Capital, for the purpose of declining with thanks an
appointment as Attorney General. "There are my probably pressing duties in North Minerva," he said in a prepared statement shaped very like a Waffle, "and besides,
there is something yukky about that job. Do you understand me? Y*u*k*k*y." He is expected to urge that the
position be abolished and that an institutional-size can of
Drano be substituted.

•

Mr. Foolfarm's health is reported to be not of the Best,
and it is thought that yesterday's Tender of the Attorney-
Generalship may be the Cause. Or it may be the alarming
Dispatches from North Minerva, where the battle against
the Eyelash Maggot is not Going Well. In any case, he is
today away in Washington, where he is advising the Vice-
President, Mr. Ford, as to certain provisions of the Hatch
Act. Mr. Foolfarm has suggested that the Vice-President
not count his Chickens until they are Hatched. The Vice-
President is alleged to have responded with Paroxysms of
Geniality.

•

"Ich dien," Mr. Foolfarm said simply, and turned away. With these words, the famed Moonshee once again left home and fireside for Washington to deal with the new Crisis. It appears that Occidental Petroleum's profits have Increased 716 percent for the first Quarter, and that the other oil companies have also done Handsomely, a fact which has occasioned Concern in some Quarters. Mr. Foolfarm's proposal is that the Government award a Bonus of 125 percent of Profits to any Company whose Gleanings have produced same in a given Time-Frame. "Profit should be rewarded," said Mr. Foolfarm, "for without profit, who would want to do all that moiling in the earth, *mon cher?"* Maggots chuckled dementedly in the grass at this remark (the phrase is the late Brian O'Nolan's) but they were our maggots thanks be to the living God and not the terrible Eyelash Maggot which has wreaked such Havoc in North Minerva.

•

Mr. Foolfarm is today in Washington for the publication of his long-awaited Novel. It is a Very Advanced Work in which three wispy Characters, identified only as "P," "E," and "H," wander about in a sort of Epistemological Hell, trying to discover what they are to Say. Sample dialogue:

P—What did I do then?

E—You understood that inaudible had unintelligible.

P—When did I understand that?

E—You understood that on the morning of the unintelligible.

P—Oh, I see. I understood that because inaudible had informed me that unintelligible.

H—Right, right. But if you understood that, at that point, then we'll have to give them the tamale grande. There's no other way.

P—The what?

H—The big tamale.

P—Oh, I see.

E—We could give them huevos rancheros.

H—Or maybe chicken mole.

E—I would just like to kind of throw this out, as a suggestion, but what about nopales con queso?

P—What?

E—Nopales con queso.

P—What is that in English?

E—Cactus.

H—They'd never bite. No, I think it's going to have to be something like frijoles refritos.

P—How do we do that?

H—You mash up a lot of beans and then fry them with, you know, your various spices.

P—But won't that look like expletive deleted?

H—It will look like you at least knew that unintelligible before inaudible and had the guts to be unintelligible.

P—I've never been afraid to be unintelligible.

E—We've never been afraid to be unintelligible.

P—That's right. I've always told everyone around here to be unintelligible.

E—And we have! We have! That's what we've got to put across.

H—Honesty is the best inaudible. Always.

P—When have I ever failed to be unintelligible?

E—You've never failed to be unintelligible.

P—What?

E—Unintelligible.

P—Oh, I see.

H—So you were inaudible then, on that date, and now you are unintelligible.

P—That's right! That's right! So that's what we'll say. And just remember one thing. What is it?

E—What is what?

P—The one thing that you're to remember.

E—I forget. Or maybe it's inaudible.

P—It *is* inaudible! *The only thing we have to inaudible is inaudible itself.*

H—That's right.

P—O.K., boys. Thank you and get a good night's unintelligible.

Mr. Foolfarm was so saddened by a reading of his own Work that he called a Press Conference and declared himself Inoperative, and has been silent as a Parsnip ever since.

Three

Heliotrope

It is April, and Heliotrope, the Open University of San Francisco, is once again turning toward the sun of felt needs and marigold-yellow fulfillments. Heliotrope is a real university, and lives at 21 Columbus Avenue, San Francisco, California, 94111. Marigold yellow is one of the colors of Heliotrope's April bulletin, on the cover of which three competition bicyclists, crash-helmeted, are bent low over their handlebars, pedaling madly toward Awareness. Come, let us join them. For too long have we tarried in the dismal sunless cities of the East. Come. Let us go, then, love, and enlist ourselves in Course D-16, Awareness and Weight Loss Workshop, designed for the

unsuccessful dieter: "Each participant will have an opportunity to tailor-make a weight-loss program incorporating
their food cravings, life-style needs, and principles of
sound nutrition. Transactional Analysis will be used as a
framework for understanding the personal motivations
that contribute to overeating problems." Come. Your
food cravings have long been a puzzlement (that time you
ordered Blue Whale Stuffed with Ford Pinto), and as for
your life style— But I am not being critical; it is the East,
the East, the Unreal City, to which I attach the blame.
That, and the stuffy rigid hierarchical closed universities
which infest it and us. Let us leave all that behind,
shoulder our backpacks, and return to basics at Heliotrope, the Open University of San Francisco. We can take
Basic Astrology, D-20: "Instructress is student of the vast
harmonious order of the universe." And so can we be, if
only we can shed our narrow paranoid pale untogether
judgmental Valium-popping Eastern ways. Required for
the course: a birth certificate or correct knowledge of
time (hour, minute), month, day, year of birth. Or we can
take Basic Bridge (D-21), Basic Macramé (D-22), Basic
Silkscreening (D-24), Basic Herb Gardening (D-111), or
Basic Turkish (D-29): "Mellow low-key course." We are
sour and high-key; that is part of what ails us—how could
we not have known? We have been frittering. Let us frit-
ter no more. Or we have been seeking answers. That is a
mistake. "When an answer is found, it is not the end but
only a beginning." Why didn't *we* think of that? The
Open University offers us beginnings and beginnings and
beginnings, and what do we want more than beginnings?
Come. We can begin Alpha & Theta Brain Wave Training (D-8), Belly Dance (D-30), Bicycle Repair and Mainte-

nance (D-31), Common Medical Problems (D-38), or Divorce Before & After (D-47). "If you are thinking about divorce, if you have recently been divorced or if you are thinking of remarriage, this is an opportunity to clarify your feelings and to share your experience with assistance from a trained professional." Who among us is not thinking about divorce, except for a few tiny-minded stick-in-the-muds who don't count? Come, love, and we will think about it together at the Open University, with assistance from a trained professional. Heliotrope, you will notice, does not offer us any untrained professionals—Heaven forfend! And if we can't clarify our feelings, perhaps we can clarify our butter, by taking Vegetarian & Natural Foods Cooking, D-102. And if these resplendent opportunities are not enough we can dip a toe into D-60, Happiness and Freedom; D-65, Hypnosis with Color; D-81, Outdoor Meditation, Intensive; D-100, Tide Pool Life; D-135, Two-Stroke Motorcycle Maintenance; D-136, Introduction to Gambling; or D-91, Stained Glass. Come, dearly beloved, hung-up, rarefied, Con Ed-haunted mandarin that you are, let us pick up our water beds and gimp off into the sunrise, to Heliotrope, the Open University of San Francisco. There is even a course in Love (D-71): "We cover self love, romantic love, humanitarian love, and spiritual love." Perhaps they know something that we do not. Ah, happy Heliotrope, with its Kung Fu, Tai Chi Chuan, Tap Dancing, Group Bioenergetic Re-education, and Gestalt for Women Over 35! Come. You, dear friend, can teach a course in Paying the Telephone Bill, and I will teach one in Napping, and we will both, at long last, be avenged upon that fancy-Dan Lionel Trilling.

And Now Let's Hear It for the Ed Sullivan Show!

The Ed Sullivan Show. Sunday night. Church of the unchurched. Ed stands there. He looks great. Not unlike an older, heavier Paul Newman. Sways a little from side to side. Gary Lewis and the Playboys have just got off. Very strong act. Ed clasps hands together. He's introducing somebody in the audience. Who is it? Ed points with his left arm. "Broken every house record at the Copa," Ed says of the man he's introducing. Who is it? It's . . . Don Rickles! Rickles stands up. Eyes glint. Applause. "I'm gonna make a big man outta you!" Ed says. Rickles hunches a shoulder combatively. Eyes glint. Applause. Jerry Vale introduced. Wives introduced. Applause.

"When Mrs. Sullivan and I were in Monte Carlo" (pause, neatly suppressed belch), "we saw them" (pause, he's talking about the next act), "for the first time and signed them instantly! The Kuban Cossacks! Named after the River Kuban!"

Three dancers appear in white fur hats, fur boots, what appear to be velvet jump suits. They're great. Terrific Cossack stuff in front of onion-dome flats. Kuban not the U.S.S.R.'s most imposing river (512 miles, shorter than the Ob, shorter than the Bug) but the dancers are remarkable. Sword dance of some sort with the band playing galops. Front dancer balancing on one hand and doing things with his feet. Great, terrific. Dancers support selves with one hand, don and doff hats with other hand. хорошó! (Non-Cyrillic approximation of Russian for "neat.") Double хорошó! Ed enters from left. Makes enthusiastic gesture with hand. Triple хорошó! Applause dies. Camera on Ed, who has hands knit before him. "Highlighting this past week in New York . . ." Something at the Garden. Can't make it out, a fight probably. Ed introduces somebody in audience. Can't see who, he's standing up behind a fat lady who's also standing up for purposes of her own. Applause.

Pigmeat Markham comes on with cap and gown and gavel. His tag line, "Here come de jedge," is pronounced and the crowd roars but not so great a roar as you might expect. The line's wearing out. Still, Pigmeat looks good, working with two or three stooges. Stooge asks Pigmeat why, if he's honest, he's acquired two Cadillacs, etc. Pigmeat says: "Because I'm very *frugal*," and whacks stooge on head with bladder. Lots of bladder work in sketch, old-timey comedy. Stooge says: "Jedge, you got to know me." Pigmeat: "Who are you?" Stooge: "I'm the man that introduced you to your wife." Pigmeat shouts, *"Life!"* and whacks the stooge on the head with the bladder. Very funny stuff, audience roars. Then a fast commercial with Jo Anne Worley from Rowan and Martin singing about Bold. Funny girl. Good commercial.

Ed brings on Doodletown Pipers, singing group. Great-looking girls in tiny skirts. Great-looking legs on girls. They sing something about "I hear the laughter" and "the sound of the future." Phrasing is excellent, attack excellent. Camera goes to atmospheric shots of a park, kids playing, mothers and fathers lounging about, a Sunday feeling. Shot of boys throwing the ball around. Shot of black baby in swing. Shot of young mother's ass, very nice. Shot of blond mother cuddling kid. Shot of black father swinging kid. Shot of a guy who looks like Rod Mc-Kuen lounging against a . . . a what? A play sculpture. But it's not Rod McKuen. The Doodletown Pipers segue into another song. Something about hate and fear, "You've got to be taught . . . hate and fear." They sound great. Shot of integrated group sitting on play equipment. Shot of young bespectacled father. Shot of young black man with young white child. He looks into camera. Thoughtful gaze. Young mother with daughter, absorbed. Nice-looking mother. Camera in tight on mother and daughter. One more mother, a medium shot. Out on shot of the tiny black child asleep in swing. Wow!

Sullivan enters from left, applauding. Makes gesture toward Pipers, toward audience, toward Pipers. Applause. Everybody's having a good time! "I want you to welcome . . . George Carlin!" Carlin is a comic. Carlin says he hates to look at the news. News is depressing.

Sample headlines: WELCOME WAGON RUNS OVER NEW-
COMER. Audience roars. PEDIATRICIAN DIES OF CHILDHOOD
DISEASE. Audience roars but a weaker roar. Carlin is
wearing a white turtleneck, dark sideburns. Joke about
youth asking father if he can use the car. Youth says he's
got a heavy date. Pa says, Then why don't you take the
pickup? Joke about the difference between organized
crime and unorganized crime. Unorganized crime is
when a guy holds you up on the street. Organized crime
is when two guys hold you up on the street. Carlin is
great, terrific, but his material is not so funny. A Central
Park joke. Cops going into the park dressed as women to
provoke molesters. Three hundred molesters arrested
and two cops got engaged. More cop jokes. Carlin holds
hands clasped together at waist. Says people wonder why
the cops don't catch the Mafia. Says have you ever tried to
catch a guy in a silk suit? Weak roar from audience. Carlin says do you suffer from nagging crime? Try the Police
Department with new improved GL-70. No roar at all. A
whicker, rather. Ed facing camera. "Coming up next . . .
right after this important word." Commercial for Royal
Electric Jetstar Typewriter. "She's typing faster and
neater now." Capable-looking woman says to camera, "I
have a Jetstar now that helps me at home where I have a
business raising St. Bernards." Behind her a St. Bernard
looks admiringly at Jetstar.

Ed's back. "England's famous Beatles" (pause, neatly
capped belch) "first appeared on our shew . . . Mary
Hopkin . . . Paul McCartney told her she must appear
on our shew . . . the world-famous . . . Mary Hopkin!"
Mary enters holding guitar. Sings something about "the
morning of my life . . . ceiling of my room . . ." Camera

in tight on Mary. Pretty blonde, slightly plump face. Heavy applause for Mary. Camera goes to black, then Mary walking away in very short skirt, fine legs, a little heavy maybe. Mary in some sort of nightclub set for her big song, "Those Were the Days." Song is ersatz Kurt Weill but nevertheless a very nice song, very nostalgic, days gone by, tears rush into eyes (mine). In the background, period stills. Shot of some sort of Edwardian group activity, possible lawn party, possible egg roll. Shot of biplane. Shot of racecourse. Camera on Mary's face. "Those were the days, my friends . . ." Shot of fox hunting, shot of tea dance. Mary is bouncing a little with the song, just barely bouncing. Shot of what appears to be a French 75 firing. Shot of lady kissing dog on nose. Shot of horse. Camera in tight on Mary's mouth. Looks like huge wad of chewing gum in her mouth but that can't be right, must be her tongue. Still of balloon ascension in background. Live girl sitting in left foreground gazing up at Mary, rapt. Mary in chaste high-collar dress with that short skirt. Effective. Mary finishes song. A real roar. Ed appears in three-quarter view turned toward the right, toward Mary. "Terrific!" Ed says. "Terrific!" Mary adjusts her breasts. "Terrific. And now, sitting out in the audience is the famous . . . Perle Mesta!" Perle stands, a contented-looking middle-aged lady. Perle bows. Applause.

Ed stares (enthralled) into camera. "Before we introduce singing Ed Ames and the first lady of the American theater, Helen Hayes . . ." A Pizza Spins commercial fades into a Tareyton Charcoal Filter commercial. Then Ed comes back to plug Helen Hayes's new book, *On Reflection*. Miss Hayes is the first lady of the American the-

ater, he says. "We're very honored to . . ." Miss Hayes
sitting at a desk, Louis-something. She looks marvelous.
Begins reading from the book. Great voice. Tons of dig-
nity. "My dear Grandchildren. At this writing, it is no
longer fashionable to have Faith; but your grandmother
has never been famous for her chic, so she isn't bothered
by the intellectual hemlines. I have always been con-
cerned with the whole, not the fragments; the positive,
not the negative; the words, not the spaces between them
. . ." Miss Hayes pauses. Hand on what appears to be a
small silver teapot. "What can a grandmother offer . . ."
She speaks very well! "With the feast of millennia set before
you, the saga of all mankind on your bookshelf . . . what
could I give you? And then I knew. Of course. My own
small footnote. The homemade bread at the banquet.
The private joke in the divine comedy. Your roots." Head
and shoulders shot of Miss Hayes. She looks up into the
lighting grid. Music up softly on, "So my grandchildren
. . . in highlights and shadows . . . bits and pieces . . .
in recalled moments, mad scenes, and acts of folly . . ."
Miss Hayes removes glasses, looks misty. "What are little
grandchildren made of . . . some good and some bad
from Mother and Dad . . . and laughs and wails from
Grandmother's tales . . . I love you." She gazes down at
book. Holds it. Camera pulls back. Music up. Applause.

Ed puts arm around Miss Hayes. Squeezes Miss Hayes.
Applause. *Heavy* applause. Ed pats hands together, join-
ing applause. Waves hands toward Miss Hayes. More
applause. It's a triumph! Ed seizes Miss Hayes's hands in
his hands. Applause dies, reluctantly. Ed says, ". . . but
first, listen to this." Shot of building, cathedral of some
kind. Organ music. Camera pans down façade past

stained-glass windows, etc. Down a winding staircase. Music changes to rock. Shot of organ keyboard. Close shot of maker's nameplate, HAMMOND. Shot of grinning organist. Shot of hands on keyboard. "The sound of Hammond starts at $599.95." Ed introduces singer Ed Ames. Ames is wearing a long-skirted coat, holding hand mike. Good eyes, good eyebrows, muttonchop sideburns. Lace at his cuffs. Real riverboat-looking. He strolls about the set singing a Tom Jones–Harvey Schmidt number, something about the morning, sometimes in the morning, something. Then another song, "it takes my breath away," "how long have I waited," something something. Chorus comes in under him. Good song. Ames blinks in a sincere way. Introduces a song from the upcoming show *Dear World*. "A lovely new song," he says. "Kiss her now, while she's young. Kiss her now, while she's yours." Set behind him looks like one-by-two's nailed vertically four inches on centers. The song is sublovely but Ames's delivery is very comfortable, easy. Chorus comes in. Ah, ah ah ah ah. Ames closes his eyes, sings something something something something; the song is submemorable. (Something memorable: early on Sunday morning a pornographic exhibition appeared mysteriously for eight minutes on television station KPLM, Palm Springs, California. A naked man and woman did vile and imaginative things to each other for that length of time, then disappeared into the history of electricity. Unfortunately, the exhibition wasn't on a network. What we really want in this world, we can't have.)

Ed enters from left (what's over there? a bar? a Barca-lounger? a book? stock ticker? model railroad?), shakes hands with Ames. Ames is much taller, but amiable. Both back out of shot, in different directions. Camera straight ahead on Ed. "Before I tell you about next week's . . . show . . . please listen to this." Commercial for Silva Thins. Then a shot of old man with ship model, commercial for Total, the vitamin cereal. Then Ed. "Next week . . . a segment from . . . the new Beatles film . . . The Beatles were brought over here by us . . . in the beginning . . . Good night!" Chopping gesture with hands to the left, to the right.

Music comes up. The crawl containing the credits is rolled over shot of Russian dancers dancing (хорошо́!). Produced by Bob Precht. Directed by Tim Kiley. Music by Ray Bloch. Associate Producer Jack McGeehan. Settings Designed by Bill Bohnert. Production Manager Tony Jordan. Associate Director Bob Schwarz. Assistant to the Producer Ken Campbell. Program Coordinator Russ Petranto. Technical Director Charles Grenier. Audio Art Shine. Lighting Director Bill Greenfield. Production Supervisor Herb Benton. Stage Managers Ed Brinkman, Don Mayo. Set Director Ed Pasternak. Costumes Leslie Renfield. Graphic Arts Sam Cecere. Talent Coordinator Vince Calandra. Music Coordinator Bob Arthur. The Ed Sullivan Show is over. It has stopped.

Bunny Image, Loss of: The Case of Bitsy S.

Four Playboy bunnies, discharged two weeks ago for having lost their "bunny image," appeared before the State Commission on Human Rights yesterday to press their complaint that Playboy practices sexual and age discrimination . . .

. . . Miss [Patti] Columbo said Tony LeMay, the "international bunny mother," told her: "You have changed from a girl to a woman. You look old. You have lost your bunny image."

"We have none of the characteristics which are considered loss of bunny image," said Nancy Phillips, one of the four. "Crinkling eyelids, sagging breasts, stretch marks, crepey necks, and drooping derrières," she said, are cited in Playboy literature as defects that will ruin the career of a bunny.

Mario Staub, general manager of the club since 1971, asserted: "Termination for bunny image has always been company practice . . . They have simply lost their bunny image—that attractive, fresh, youthful look they had when they started."

—*The New York Times*

Introduction

Loss of bunny image, or Staub's syndrome, was first identified as a distinct clinical entity by Altmann. Bunny image, or the plastic representation of one's corporeal self as differentiated in specific ways from the corporeal selves of others, was discussed by Steinem and others as early as 1963. But it was Altmann who refined the concept and, more particularly, the cluster of pathologies associated with its loss. It is true that Altmann's work is indebted to that of Pick, whose valuable discussion of the phenomenon of the "phantom limb" following amputation provided, as Altmann has acknowledged, a fruitful hint. But it was the case of Bitsy S., the protocol of which follows, that gave this investigator his most important insights, and his place in the literature of body disturbances.

Case Report

Bitsy S., an attractive white female of twenty-eight, was admitted to Bellevue Hospital complaining that she could not find, physically locate, her own body. It was "gone," she said, and added that she needed it and wanted it back. She further said that she had looked everywhere for it, that it was absolutely nowhere to be found, and that she had thought of going to the police about the matter but had decided instead to resort to the hospital because she felt that the police might think she was "strange." The case was first diagnosed as one of simple amnesia, but when the patient did not respond to routine procedures (including hypnosis), Altmann was consulted.

Altmann began with a series of questions.

(Investigator grasps left hand of patient, bringing it to patient's eye level.)

"What is this?"

"A hand."

"Right or left?"

(Patient examines hand carefully.)

"Left."

"Whose hand is it?"

"I don't know."

"To what is the hand attached?"

(Patient studies hand and forearm.)

"Arm."

"Whose arm?"

"I don't know."

"Is it your arm?"

"No. I don't have an arm."

(Investigator gently moves his hand up the arm in a series of light touches, finally coming to rest on the patient's left shoulder.)

"What is this?"

"Shoulder."

"Your shoulder?"

"No. I don't have a shoulder."

"*Somebody's* shoulder."

(The patient considers this for a moment.)

"Probably. Maybe."

(The investigator squeezes the shoulder slightly—a friendly squeeze.)

The subject then said, in a singsong voice:

"Please, sir, you are not allowed to touch the Bunnies."

This was, of course, Altmann's first clue. In connection with his studies of horror vacui he had quite naturally gravitated toward the New York Playboy Club and had, in fact, been a keyholder since its inception. Thus the statement "Please, sir, you are not allowed to touch the Bunnies" was not an unfamiliar one. He immediately asked:

"Are you a Bunny?"

"No," she said. "I am not a Bunny."

"If you are not a Bunny then why are you a member of the class of persons that I am not allowed to touch?"

There was no response from the patient.

"Were you ever a Bunny?"

"Yesterday."

"You were a Bunny yesterday?"

"Yesterday I was a Bunny and today I am not a Bunny. I was terminated. For loss of bunny image."

"What is 'bunny image'?"

"The attractive, fresh, youthful look I had when I started. The International Bunny Mother came to me and said: 'You have changed from a girl into a woman. You look old. You have lost your bunny image.' Then she cut off my bunny tail, with a pair of tin snips. Then she asked for my ears back. I gave her my ears back. I was weeping. I asked her why. That was a mistake. She told me. Crinkling eyelids. Crepey neck. Drooping derrière. I mentioned that I had been pinched thrice on that derrière the night before. She said that that was not enough, that I was below the national average for pinches-per-night. I said that I slept every night in a bathtub filled to the brim with Skin Life, by Helena Rubinstein. She said that she appreciated my 'desire' but that it was time to cut the squad and the rookies coming up from the farm clubs were growing impatient. I said I would stuff extra Kleenex into the top of my bunny costume, if that would help. She said that some people just didn't know when it was time to hang it up. Loss of bunny image, she said, was more than a physical thing. There were intangibles involved. I asked for an example of an intangible. She looked out of the window and said she had to catch a plane for Chicago. And then this morning I woke up and couldn't find my body. It was gone. Naturally I looked in the mirror first but there was nothing in the mirror—just mirror. Then I tried to touch my toes but when I tried to touch my toes there were no toes and no fingers to touch them with. Then I began to get worried."

(The investigator then complimented the patient warmly on her physical appearance, which was in fact, as noted above, quite feminine, attractive, and pleasing.)

"Who are you talking about?" she asked.

"You."

"You is lost," she said. "Somewhere all the lost bunny images are, each Bunny calling for its Bunny Mother, each lost bunny image still somewhere stuffing plastic laundry bags into the bosom of its bunny costume, bunny tails still pert, white, oh so white, each lost bunny image still practicing the Bunny Stance, the Bunny Dip—"

The investigator then began a course of Teddy Bear therapy, in which the subject is gradually introduced to an object which is not the subject but which holds in common with the subject certain physical features (arms, legs, head, etc.) which, in time, enable the patient to "find" himself—in this instance, herself—by equating the specific appurtenances of the teddy bear with his or her own body parts. Although this course of treatment shamelessly trades upon the natural love of human beings for teddy bears, it was felt that it was not in essence more manipulative than other therapies. A more dangerous contraindication was, of course, the unfortunate parity between "bunny" and "teddy bear"—the problems involved being obvious. Altmann nevertheless decided that it was the therapy of choice and its use was validated by the fact that Bitsy S. has once again "found" her own body and, indeed, has been able to construct a mature, stable, and "giving" relationship with a member of the medical profession.

Conclusion

The life of man, as Vince Lombardi said, is nasty, brutish, and short.

The Expedition

We mustered on May 9, 1873, at Salinas, California. We were 206 men and 14 officers.

Colonel Goudy

Major MacDennis
—a good man.
He later died on
the ice.

This was fabricated specially for the expedition.

Saying goodbye to Birdie was one of the hardest things I have ever done.

Just before we sailed a couple of the boys got into a pretty good shindy. Captain Ross broke it up.

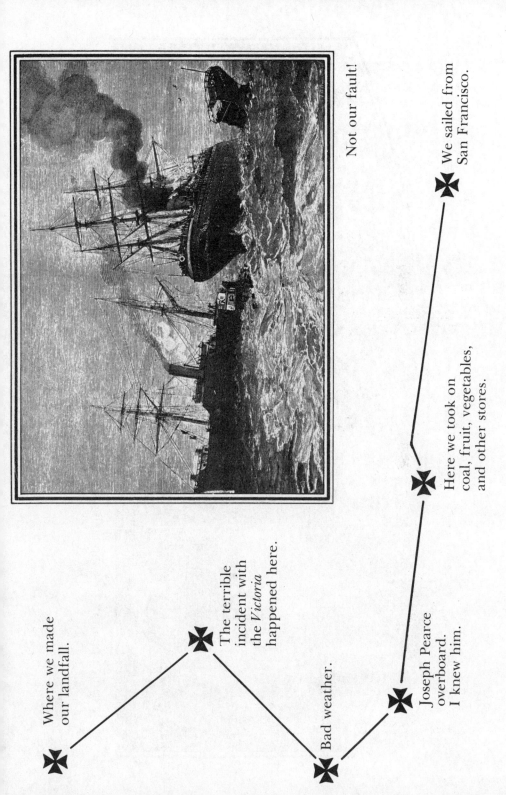

Not our fault!

We sailed from
San Francisco.

Here we took on
coal, fruit, vegetables,
and other stores.

The terrible
incident with
the *Victoria*
happened here.

Where we made
our landfall.

Bad weather.

Joseph Pearce
overboard.
I knew him.

It became apparent that the navigator, Lieutenant Petrie, was less than competent. He was replaced.

After we left the ship we had some cold nights.

The ice caves were a singular and awesome sight. Colonel
Goudy pressed on. Then, on March 13, 1874 . . .

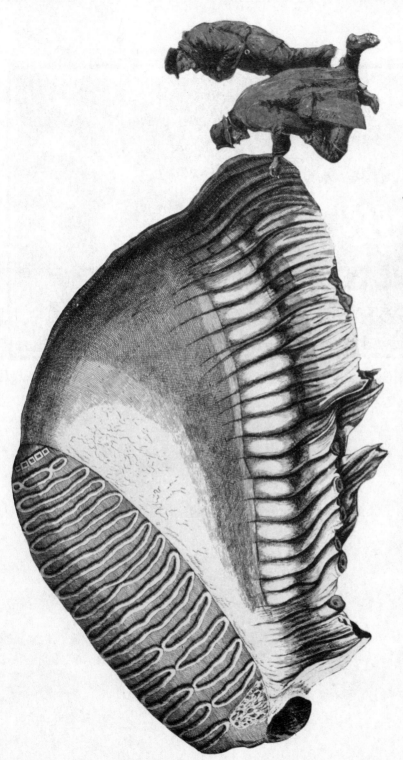

We found it! The largest one of its kind ever discovered.

The team that made the actual "find." I am third from left, rear row.

There was a lot of excitement when we got back. This is the parade.
The Vice-President spoke.

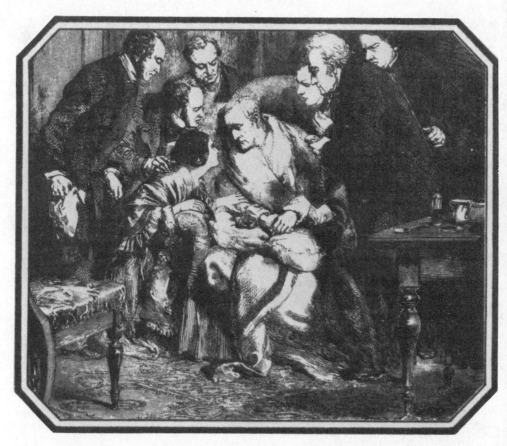

Brigadier General Goudy passed away on December 1, 1889.

Games Are the Enemies of Beauty, Truth, and Sleep, Amanda Said

I was playing Password, Twister, Breakthru, Bonanza, Stratego, Squander, and Gambit. And Quinto, Phlounder, Broker, Tactics, and Stocks & Bonds. All at once. On the floor. It was my move. When I play alone, it is always my move. That is reasonable. I kneel first on one side of the board, then the other. I think a bit, I examine my move to make sure it is the correct move. I congratulate myself. Then I hobble to the next board, on my knees.

The floor of my study is covered with game boards, and there are boards in the bedroom, the kitchen, the bath. Conestoga, the Game of the Oregon Trail. Gettysburg, Stalingrad, Midway, D-Day, U-Boat, Bismarck, and

Waterloo. Le Mans. Management, Verdict, and Dispatcher. Merger, the Game of Stock Manipulation in the Automobile Industry. Qubic, the 3-D Tic Tac Toe Game. My move. It is my move when I depart for the office in the morning and my move when I return at night. I move before, during, and after dinner, hobbling from board to board. It is my move when I go to bed and my move when I awake.

I extended an arm in its yellow vinyl smoking jacket. I moved. Then I hobbled around to the other side of the board to evaluate the move from the point of view of my opponent. A foolish move. Now I was in a position to destroy myself. Should I destroy myself?

Then the bell rang. It was Amanda. She was in tears. "Amanda," I said. "What is it?" She was wearing a tent dress, two-ply brown canvas with a tent-peg trim. Her eyes were full of sparklers and tears.

"Oh, Hector," she said. "You are the only one who can help me. Something awful—"

"Is it the same old thing?"

"No," she said. "It is a new thing. It is the worst thing you can imagine."

"Come," I said. "Stay with me. Take this buffalo robe and wrap it around your tent dress. And have a shot of this apricot brandy, and sit down here in this comfortable chair in front of the thermostat."

"I was playing Afrika Korps," she said. "You know Afrika Korps. A re-creation of the famed exploits of Field Marshal Rommel. You command the actual units and introduce the original divisions, brigades, and regiments at the actual time of their arrival, according to the actual historical situation."

"I know. One is given an opportunity to display one's generalship, strategic grasp, and tactical sense."

"Right," Amanda said, knocking back a bit of the brandy. "Well, when I came home this evening—Hector, I can't describe it! An entire Army Group had mixed itself up with the pieces from my Water Polo game. And the battleships from Midway have drifted into the Verdict box, and all the stock shares from Merger, the Game of Stock Manipulation in the Automobile Industry, are scrambled up with the counters from Depression, and—Hector, why am I playing all these *games*? Card games, word games, board games, educational games, and games people play? What is it, Hector? Is there something strange about me? Am I some kind of a creepy nut freak? I seem to spend all my time—"

I took her hand with its four-inch orange, yellow, and blue papier-mâché Fish & Game Commission ring.

"Amanda," I said. "You are not alone. Everyone is playing these games. Everyone I know." I took her to the window and opened it. We stuck our heads out into the papier-mâché night. "Listen, Amanda."

She listened. "What is that sort of funny thrimp-thrimp sound? Thrimp thrimp thrimp thrimp thrimp thrimp?"

"That is the sound made by the nation's terrific and gigantic electronic computers pulsing," I said. "Of which there are now perhaps thirty-five thousand in use, from sea to shining sea. It is estimated that there will be eighty-five thousand of them in use by 1975. And a substantial portion of these computers are playing games, Amanda, even as you and I. The businessmen are playing Daddy Warbucks games, the Lost Horse game for example, in order to establish patterns that will enable them to man-

gle the competition. The military men are playing war
games, Escalation for example, in order to test the ef-
ficacy of alternate responses to the provocations of the
enemy. And to make new enemies, for all I know. The
scientists are playing scientific games, and some people
are playing plain old checkers. And Marshall McLuhan
says that games are dramatic modes of our psychological
lives, providing release for particular tensions in social
groups. And Huizinga says that the play element in culture serves a civilizing function, combining an agonistic
principle of competitiveness with a ludic principle, or
pure play. And Shub in his *Game Theory and Related Ap-
proaches to Social Behavior . . .*"

"Yes," Amanda said, "but what about me? My head is
full of Diplomacy, and my heart is full of Careers. And
my hands are full of Hoodwink, and my bank account is
full of Monopoly money. I'm exhausted, Hector. I'm *tired*
of playing games. I want—"

"I know," I said. "Relax, Amanda. We can lick this
thing. Just trust me."

"What do you propose?" she asked, her brilliant aqua
eyes full of fondness and eye shadow. "What?"

"New games," I said. "New games, Amanda, to set the
turkey of mental excitement flying through the thin air of
intellectual irresponsibility."

"New games?" I noticed that the blood had run out of
her face. But I could not see where it had gone. "You
mean people can make up their own games? Isn't that
. . . hubris?"

"Have another brandy," I said. "Have another brandy
and we will play Contretemps, the Game of Social Embarrassment. And Cofferdam, and Double Boiler, and

Hubris too, if you like. Listen to the names of these glorious new games—Leftwards, Gearbox, Dentist's Appointment, and Stroke. We will invent them together, dear friend."

"How is this game played? Contretemps or whatever it is?"

"I'm glad you asked me that question," I said, "because I know the answer. One starts with a situation, a social situation. One with a potential for embarrassment. One in which one is a bit out of one's depth, so to say. Then the potential is actualized. Imagine for instance that you are attending a lavish reception at the Court of St. James's. You have just converted your holdings in sterling, which were vast, into Siamese baht. In consequence, the Queen's allowance has been cut. You notice that she is wearing last year's tiara. You step up to be presented. You notice that she is staring at you with a funny expression on her face."

"Not bad," Amanda said. "Give me another one."

"Okay. A more elaborate one. You are attending a lavish reception at the Court of St. James's. Present also is Lord Snowdon, husband of Princess Margaret and famous photographer. The editor of the *Sunday Times* color—that should be colour—magazine is there too. Lord Snowdon has been on assignment for the magazine. He is doing a picture story on—"

"The Stones."

"Very good. He is doing a picture story on the Stones. Lord Snowdon is showing his prints to the editor. You are looking over their shoulders. As it happens, you too have recently taken some colour shots of the Stones. With your old box camera."

"Your old box camera that was your great-grand-mother's that you found in an old trunk in the attic and that is held together with masking tape," Amanda said.

"Superb. Whereas Lord Snowdon has been shooting with a pair of matched Hasselblads with four-thousand-dollar lenses. You regard Lord Snowdon's pictures over the editor's shoulder. Then you reach into your reticule and withdraw your own pictures. 'These are terrible,' you say, 'but I thought you might just . . .' The editor gazes intently at your photographs. He drops Lord Snowdon's photographs on the floor. 'By God,' the editor says. 'You mean you . . . with your great-grandmother's camera held together with masking tape . . .' Lord Snowdon is staring at you with a funny expression on his face."

"Quelle horreur!" Amanda murmured.

"That is Contretemps," I said. "The situations tend to get more and more elaborate and horrible. A particularly good game for self-punishment, if that is what you crave. The situation in which you are in the studio of a famous artist, one who paints pitiful little girls with big eyes, and your own child, come to have her portrait done, refuses to open her eyes at all—that one is rather stimulating, I must say. And there are others. You are on the operating table. You are draped with a white sheet. You have bor-rowed a kidney from a friend. Now it is time to return it. The doctor—"

"More games," Amanda said. "More games and more brandy."

"We could play Broadway Flop," I said. "The Game of Ill-Conceived Musical Comedy. One attempts to construct the particular work least likely to get out of New Haven alive. A Lionel Bart musical based on *The Waste Land,* for example. Titled *Wasteland!* At the finale, Albert and Lil decide to leave Rats' Alley and make a new start in America. Or we could play Bag, the History of Jazz Game. The object of the game is to bring jazz up the river from New Orleans. Conflict provided by evil commercial-music interests who want to stop the spread of the New Thing. The evil commercial-music interests represented on the board by—"

"Squares," Amanda said triumphantly, and I gathered her into my arms. Then we played Famous Last Words, the Game of Deathbed Utterances, locked in a lovers' embrace on the fire escape. People down below stood agape, hanging upon the tense exchange between us.

"It is enough," I said.

"Immanuel Kant," she said.

"If there is no question, there is no answer."

"Gertrude Stein."

"This is a fickle and faithless generation."

"Captain Kidd."

"Bertie."

"Queen Victoria."

"I do not understand what I have to do."

"Leo Tolstoy."

"Hang on to the Matchless; it will make millions again."

"I can't remember, I can't remember!"

"Tabor the Silver King," I said. "Didn't you see *The Ballad of Baby Doe?*"

"These games are marvelous," Amanda said. "I like them especially because they are so meaningless and boring, and trivial. These qualities, once regarded as less than desirable, are now everywhere enthroned as the key elements in our psychological lives, as reflected in the art of the period as well as—"

"Yes," I said. Then we played:

Crise du Cinéma, in which one improves existing films by supplying new casting and variant endings (Doris Day for Ingrid Bergman in *For Whom the Bell Tolls;* after El Sordo's band is wiped out, Maria persuades Robert Jordan to settle with her in a nice suburb of Barcelona).

Zen Zen (pointless answers are given to simple questions. "Where is the Administration Building?" "Ha, ha. Your hat is falling off." Blows are exchanged).

Break the Ball (an accumulation of balls from ball games—footballs, baseballs, basketballs, tennis balls, cricket balls—is demolished, using a twelve-pound sledge).

"What comes after Break the Ball?" Amanda asked.

"After the Ball Is Over. A fine game played with an empty punchbowl and four hundred overcoats. You attempt to find your overcoat in the pile of overcoats. You are forbidden to use your hands, feet, or teeth. Or anybody else's hands, feet, or teeth."

"Games are the enemies of beauty, truth, and sleep," Amanda said. The brandy was almost gone.

"There remains one more game."

"What is it?"

"Ennui," I said. "The easiest of all. No rules, no boards, no equipment."

"What is Ennui?" Amanda asked, setting it up for me.

"Ennui is the absence of games," I said, "the modern world at its most vulnerable." But she had folded her tent dress and silently stolen away.

A Nation of Wheels

With the invention of vulcanization by Goodyear in 1839, it became possible to obtain a rubber that retained a high degree of resilience over a wide range of temperatures. This development had its most important application in the rubber automobile tire. America quickly became *a nation of wheels*.

Originally linked to the internal-combustion engine to provide cheap individual transportation, the wheel assumed near-autonomous status in the 1970's with the arrival of (1) self-powering devices and (2) the so-called "elastic consciousness."

The interface of man and machine had long before produced a sort of shared mental activity. The human factor had been, however, dominant. Men had been "calling the shots." But now a product of technology had developed "a mind of its own." Human factors found this disquieting in the extreme.

It rapidly became clear that a technological revolution of an order of magnitude beyond anything previously imaginable had taken place. Moreover, behavior of the revolutionaries tended to be distressingly value-free. A number of "incidents" were recorded.

First manifestation of the wheel's new self-regard was the sudden appearance, in every area of the country, of hundreds of Welcome Wagons that seemed to be directed by no human agency. These, with implacable good will, carried warm greetings into every American home. But from whom?

Tradition-oriented individuals sounded the alarm.

Other individuals were quickly co-opted.

All defenses were found to be penetrable.

Resistance ended. The streets belonged to the wheels. Human beings ventured out of their homes only with the greatest timidity. A committee of wheels met to formulate a list of non-negotiable demands. A spokesman said, "Guidance of the Vehicle of State requires the most subtle intelligence the culture offers. We want a wheel at the wheel." The new President was acclaimed by nearly everyone.

People who had, in the past, suffered from technophobia suffered even more. Others took other positions. Things were not so bad. Things could be worse. Worse things could be imagined. Worse things had been endured, and triumphed over, in the past. This was not the worst. The worst was yet to come.

A few hotheads engaged in acts of defiance. These acts, the wheels said, were "D'Artagnanistic" and objectively useless. A technological revolution, they explained, cannot be successfully resisted. It can only be supplanted, by another technological revolution.

Nevertheless, the secret police were everywhere.

What the wheels wanted, and obtained, was *Lebensraum*. Structures of all kinds were demolished to provide more space for freeways, throughways, parkways, and expressways. Parking lots proliferated. Soon entire cities were being bulldozed into rubble to make way for miles and miles of new concrete.

Finally, only a thin ribbon of human space remained, running from Augusta, Maine, to San Diego, California, and bound on both sides by limitless savannas of gray.

The Departure from Baltimore.

The inevitable work of rewriting the history of the culture proceeded apace. "America is *based on* the wheel," the President said, "and furthermore, it always was." The museums mysteriously filled with artifacts supporting this thesis.

The Venus of Akron.

A class in wheel appreciation.

Human beings, nose-to-nose in their tiny spaces, reacted in predictable ways: "Things could be worse." "Worse things could be imagined." "This is not the worst." "The worst is yet to come." Propinquity was redefined as desirable, lack of space as a higher good. "Tight is right," people said.

But now stretches of pavement have been heard whispering to each other.

"Why wheels?" they say.

"What do we need them for?"

"A perfectly paved globe . . ."

Two Hours to Curtain

A big battle dance in Rogers, Tennessee! These country boys, despised and admired, know what they're about. The way they pull on their strings—the strings of their instruments, and the strings of their fates. Bringing up the bass line here, inserting "fills" there, in their expensive forty-dollar Western shirts and plain ordinary nine-dollar jeans. Four bands are competing, and the musicians backstage are unscrewing their flasks and tasting the bourbon inside, when they are not lighting their joints and pipes and hookahs. Meanwhile they're looking over the house, the Masonic Temple, a big pile of stone erected in 1928, and wondering whether the wiring will

be adequate to the demands of their art. The flasks and
joints are being passed around, and everyone is wiping
his mouth on his sleeve. And so the ropes holding the
equipment to the roofs of the white station wagons are
untied, and the equipment is carried onto the stage, with
its closed curtain and its few spotty work lights shining.
The various groups send out for supper, ordering steak
sandwiches on a bun, hold the onions or hold the lettuce,
as individual taste dictates. The most junior member of
each group or a high-ranking groupie goes over to the
café with the list, an envelope on which all the orders
have been written, and reads off the orders to the counterman there, and the counterman says, "You with the
band?" and the go-for says, "Yup," succinct and not putting too fine a point on it. Meanwhile the ushers have arrived, all high-school girls who are members of the
Daughters of the Mystic Shrine Auxiliary, wearing white
blouses and blue miniskirts, with a red sash slung across
their breasts and tied at the hip, a badge of office. These,
the flower of Rogers's young girls, all go backstage to ad-
mire the musicians, and this is their privilege, because the
performance doesn't begin for another hour, and they
stand around looking at the musicians, and the musicians
look back at them, and certain thoughts push their way
into all of the minds gathered there, under the work
lights, but then are pushed out again, because there is
music to be performed this night! and one of the ampli-
fiers has just blown its slo-blo fuse, and nobody can remember where the spare fuses were packed, and also the
microphones provided by the Temple are freaking out,
and in addition the second band's drummer discovers
that his heads are soggy (probably as a result of that situa-

tion outside Tulsa, where the bridge was out and the station wagon more or less forded the river), but luckily he
has brought along a hot plate to deal with this sort of con-
tingency, and he plugs it in and begins toasting his heads,
to bring them back to the right degree of brashness for
the performance. And now the first people are filling up
the seats, out in front of the curtain, some of them sitting
in seats that are better, strictly speaking, than those they
had paid for, in the hopes that the real owners of the
seats will not show up, having been detained by a medical
emergency. All of the musicians take turns in looking out
over the auditorium through a hole in the closed curtain,
counting the house and looking for girls who are especially beautiful. And now the M.C. arrives, a very jovial
man in a big white Western hat, such as the Stetson company has stopped making, and he goes around shaking
hands with everybody, cutting up old touches, and the
musicians tolerate this, because it is a part of their life.
And now everybody is tuning up, and you hear parts of
lots of different songs, fragments clashing with each
other, because each musician has a different favorite bit
that he likes to tune up with, although sometimes two
musicians will start in on the same piece at the same time,
because they are thinking alike, at that moment. And now
the hall is filling up with people who are well- or ill-
dressed, according to the degree that St. Pecula has
smiled upon them, and the Daughters of the Mystic Shrine
are outside, with their programs, which contain advertise-
ments from the Bart Lumber Yard, and the Sons and
Daughters of I Will Arise, and the House of Blue Lights,
and the Sunbeam Vacuum Cleaner Company, and the
Okay Funeral Home. A man comes backstage with a

piece of paper on which is written the order in which the
various performers will appear. The leaders of the
various groups drift over to this man and look at his piece
of paper, to see what spot on the bill has been given to
each band, while the bandsmen talk to each other, in enthusiastic or desultory fashion, according to their natures.
"Where'd you git that shirt?" "Took it off a cop in Tex-
arkana." "How much you give for it?" "Dollar and a half."
And now everybody is being careful not to drink too
much, because drinking too much slows down your attack, and if there is one thing you don't want in this kind
of situation it is having your attack slowed down. Of
course some people are into drinking and smoking a lot
more before they play, but that's another idea, and now
the audience on the other side of the closed curtain is a
loud presence, and everyone has the feeling of something
important about to happen, and the first band to perform
gets into position, with the three guitar players in a kind
of skirmish line in front, the drummer spread out behind
them, and the electric-piano player off to the side somewhat, more or less parallel to the drummer, and the
happy M.C. standing in front of the guitar players, with
his piece of paper in his hand, and the stage manager
looking alternately at his watch and at the people out
front. One of the musicians borrows a last cigarette from
another musician, and all of the musicians are fiddling
with the controls of their instruments, and the drummer
is tightening his snares, and the stage manager says
"O.K." to the M.C., and the M.C. holds up his piece of
paper and prepares to read what is written there into the
bunch of microphones before him, and the houselights
go down as the stage lights come up, and the M.C. looks

at the leader of the first group, who nods complacently, and the M.C. shouts into the microphones (from behind the closed curtains) in a hearty, dramatic voice, *"From Rogers, Tennessee, the Masonic Temple Battle of the Bands, it's Bill Tippey and the Happy Valley Boys!"* and the band crashes into "When Your Tender Body Touches on Mine," and the curtains part, and the crowd goes crazy.

The Photographs

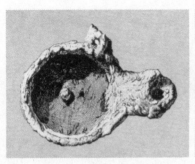

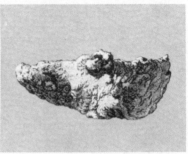

FIG. 1   FIG. 2

The attached photographs of the human soul (Figs. 1 and 2), taken by Pioneer 10, the first spacecraft to navigate the outer solar system, were made on December 14, 1973, as the craft was leaving the magnetic field of Jupiter. The "photographs" (actually coded radio signals from the device's nine-foot dish antenna beamed back to earth) were, of course, incidental to the photographing of Jupiter itself, one of the mission's chief aims. They were made by Dr. Reginald Hobson, F.R.S., of Britain's Cavendish Laboratory, using Kodak spectroscopic plates type IIIa-J baked for five hours at 65° C. under dry N_2 before exposure. Dr. Hobson very shortly afterward brought the resulting images to his friend and colleague Dr. Winston Watnick-Mealie, F.R.S.

"Uh, Winnie—"

"Yes, Reggie?"

"I have something to show you."

"More shots from 10?"

"Right, Winnie. But these . . . There's something rather special about them."

"What's that, Reggie?"

"Well, Winnie, I have reason to believe that they are photographs of the human soul on its way to Heaven."

"Oh, really. That's *interesting*. Photographs of the human soul on its way to Heaven. I suppose you've, uh, checked this out, have you, Reggie? I mean—"

"Uh—rather thoroughly, Winnie. I did a computer search of all extant images from space, and, uh, these photographs are *sui generis,* you might say. They are like nothing previously photographed. Nothing. I also did a worm-path study of the possibilities, and the result of the worm-path study was that, uh, these *can only be* photographs of the human soul on its way to Heaven."

"Any other tests?"

"Fourier analysis. Critical-band masking. Continuous smearing grids."

"Um. Well, then, I suppose that's that, isn't it? You're quite sure it's the *soul*—the human soul?"

"Worm-path studies don't lie, Winnie. I ran the program four times."

"The human soul . . . on its way to, ah, Heaven."

"One assumes. It was definitely outward bound."

"I see. Well, then, let's have a look at them."

"Right here, Winnie."

"God. Ugly little bugger, isn't it."

"Not precisely pretty. I wouldn't, for example, call it gorgeous."

"Definitely not gorgeous. Rather unattractive, actually."

"I remarked that myself."

"Looks rather like a frying pan."

"Yes, it does, rather."

"A heavily, uh, corroded frying pan. You see that handle sort of part, over to the right."

"Yes, I noticed that. Looks rather like a, ah, handle."

"A bit used-looking, the whole thing."

"Quite."

"And then there's that, ah, knuckle sort of thing there at the top. What d'you make of that, Reggie?"

"Haven't the faintest, Winnie. What you might call an anomaly."

"Yes, definitely anomalous. I mean, one doesn't like to think of souls, the human soul, as having . . . knuckle-shaped things sticking out at the top, does one?"

"Much prefer not, Winnie. It bothered me, too."

"Yes. It's disturbing."

"Yes. Definitely disturbing."

"I always thought of the soul as being more . . . *symmetrical,* don't you know."

"Right. Sort of . . . beautiful. Like that stuff one puts on the Christmas tree at Christmas. What's it called?"

"Angel hair."

"Right. Sort of like angel hair. Ethereal."

"Ethereal, that's the ticket. And now to see it looking very much like something someone's been frying eggs and kidneys and God knows what all in for just ages and ages—well it sort of takes the wind out of one's sails, as it were."

"Very disturbing, I agree, Winnie."

"I wonder what that little nipple-shaped business is, in the middle there."

"Yes, I was curious, too. Probably should be looked into."

"Why couldn't it have been, you know, *beautiful?* If you follow me."

"Well, there *is* sin and all that, of course."

"Yes. Sin. I was afraid you were going to mention that."

"I don't quite follow."

"Well, the thing is, Reggie, I have something to confess. Something in the sin line, actually."

"Something to confess?"

"Yes. I don't know quite how to put it, but it's something that's been rather on my mind, these past weeks."

"What ever are you talking about?"

"Well, it's about Dorothea."

"Dorothea?"

"Yes, Dorothea. The thing is, I ran into Dorothea a few months ago. At Marks & Spencer. She was looking for some orange thread."

"Yes, for her tatting."

"Yes. She was tatting a bedspread, I believe. An orange bedspread."

"Yes, she's finished it. It's on the bed now, in the bedroom."

"Quite. Well, Dorothea was looking for some orange thread—a particular shade of orange—"

"Yes. It's called burnt orange, Winnie. A sort of burnt-looking orange."

"Right. Well, she, as I say, was looking for this special shade of orange thread, and *I* was looking for a thimble."

"You were looking for a thimble."

"Right. Margaret had asked me to stop off at Marks & Spencer and fetch her home a thimble. She'd lost her thimble."

"I see."

"I bought two, actually. In case she misplaced one, she'd have the other, you see. Sort of a back-up system."

"Um."

"Well, as it happens the thimble department is quite close to the thread department, at Marks & Spencer. They're adjacent."

"I should think they'd be pretty well the same department."

"One would think that, but as it happens they're separate departments. Separate, but adjacent. So I sort of ran into Dorothea, that afternoon, and in the ordinary way asked her if she'd like to pop out for a drink."

"She accepted."

"Ah, yes. So we popped out and had a drink. Several, in fact."

"I see."

"And, uh, one thing sort of led to another, and the fact is that I've been seeing quite a bit of Dorothea in the past weeks. Illicitly."

"Illicitly."

"Yes. Behavior which is, strictly speaking, non-licit."

"Um. And you've been feeling a bit uneasy about it?"

"Yes. Horrid, in fact."

"Well, I can understand that, Winnie. It is a bit sticky, given the fact that we've been friends and colleagues all these years. Since the fifties, really."

"The late fifties, yes. I came here in 1956."

"But I don't quite see, Winnie, what this has to do with these photographs. Of the human soul on its way to Heaven. The first ever. I would say that the immediate problem is not your little flutter with my wife, Dorothea, but the photographs. I mean, business before pleasure, Winnie."

"Right, Reggie. I couldn't agree more. You always were one for getting on with it."

"The question is, in my view, what are we to do with the bloody things?"

"Burn them."

"Burn them? But they are of some scientific interest, wouldn't you say? I mean, if the soul exists, and we have the snaps to prove it, it would have quite a lot of relevance, wouldn't it? To everything?"

"Well, yes, I suppose it would have *some* relevance. Give the theologians a hell of a fright, for one thing. Might be worth publishing, just for that reason."

"Yes, I can see that."

"Of course, on the other hand, a great many people— decent, serious people—are probably *very interested* in this sort of thing. The existence of the human soul. I mean, it's not like the tooth fairy, right?"

"Much more relevance, I'd say, Winnie. To things in general."

"Well, Reggie, it's what you might call a nice question. There's our responsibility to science and truth and all that. But aren't we sort of in the position of those chaps who made the atom bomb and then were sorry afterward?"

"Yes, I'd say we were, actually. Rather."

"It seems to me to boil down to this: Are we better off *with* souls, or just possibly *without* them?"

"Yes. I see what you mean. You prefer the uncertainty."

"Exactly. It's more creative. Take for example my, ah, arrangement with your wife, Dorothea. Stippled with uncertainty. At moments, we are absolutely *quaking* with nonspecific anxiety. *I* enjoy it. *Dorothea* enjoys it. The humdrum is defeated. Momentarily, of course."

"Yes, I can understand that. Gives the thing a bit of zest."

"Yes. You'd be taking away people's zest. They'd all have to go around being good and all that. You'd get the Nobel Prize, and no one, repeat *no one,* would ever speak to you again. People do like their zest, Reggie."

"But still—"

"There's just one more item, Reggie. One more item to be considered. I am absolutely persuaded that you have succeeded in capturing the first hard evidence for the existence of the human soul. But it's flawed."

"The thing *is* a bit on the homely side."

"Downright ugly, to be perfectly frank."

"God knows what a life it must have led."

"Yes, but don't you see, Reggie, that these snaps, if they are published, will come to stand for, in the public mind, *all souls?*"

"I suppose there's something in that."

"Some things it's better not to know about. That's what I'm suggesting."

"Your affair with Dorothea would be an example."

"An *excellent* example, Reggie."

"Of course there is some fallout from all this. The affair, I mean."

"What is that, Reggie?"

"I don't like you any more, Winnie."

"Yes, I should think you'd have that reaction, Reggie. Quite normal, I'd say."

"So I'll burn the photographs, I expect."

"Yes. Pity they weren't prettier."

"Yes. Pity they weren't prettier."

Nothing:
A Preliminary Account

It's not the yellow curtains. Nor curtain rings. Nor is it bran in a bucket, not bran, nor is it the large, reddish farm animal eating the bran from the bucket, the man who placed the bran in the bucket, his wife, or the raisin-faced banker who's about to foreclose on the farm. None of these is nothing. A damselfish is not nothing, it's a fish, a *Pomacentrus,* it likes warm water, coral reefs—perhaps even itself, for all we know. Nothing is not a nightshirt or a ninnyhammer, ninety-two, or Nineveh. It is not a small jungle in which, near a river, a stone table has been covered with fruit. It is not the handsome Indian woman standing next to the stone table holding the blond, kidnapped child. Neither is it the proposition *esse est percipi*, nor is it any of the refutations of that proposition. Nor is it snuff. Hurry. There is not much time, and we must complete, or at least attempt to complete, the list. Nothing is not a tongue depressor; splendid, hurry on. Not a tongue depressor on which a distinguished artist has painted part of a nose, part of a mouth, a serious, unsmiling eye. Good, we got that in. Hurry on. We are persuaded that nothing is not the yellow panties. The yellow panties edged with white on the floor under the black chair. And it's not the floor or the black chair or the two naked lovers standing up in the white-sheeted bed having a pillow fight during the course of which the male partner will, unseen by his beloved, load his pillowcase with a copy of Webster's Third International. We are nervous. There is not much time. Nothing is not a Gregorian chant or indeed a chant of any kind unless it be the howl of the null muted to inaudibility by the laws of language strictly construed. It's not an "O" or an ampersand or what Richard is thinking or that thing we can't name at the moment but which we use to clip papers together. It's not the ice cubes disappearing in the warmth of our whiskey nor is it the town in Scotland where the whiskey is manufactured nor is it the workers who, while reading the Bible and the local newspaper and Rilke, are sentiently sipping the product through eighteen-foot-long, almost invisible nylon straws.

And it's not a motor hotel in Dib (where the mudmen live) and it's not pain or *pain* or the mustard we spread on the *pain* or the mustard plaster we spread on the pain, fee simple, the roar of fireflies mating, or meat. Nor is it lobster protected from its natural enemies by its high price or true grit or false grit or thirst. It's not the yellow curtains, we have determined that, and it's not what is behind the yellow curtains which we cannot mention out of respect for the King's rage and the Queen's reputation. Hurry. Not much time. Nothing is not a telephone number or any number whatsoever including zero. It's not science and in particular it's not black-hole physics, which is not nothing but physics. And it's not (quickly now, quickly) Benjamin Franklin trying to seduce, by mail, the widow of the French thinker Claude Adrien Helvétius, and it is not the nihilism of Gorgias, who asserts that nothing exists and even if something did exist it could not be known and even if it could be known that knowledge could not be communicated, no, it's not that although the tune is quite a pretty one. I am sorry to say that it is not Athos, Porthos, or Aramis, or anything that ever happened to them or anything that may yet happen to them if, for example, an Exxon tank truck exceeding the speed limit outside of Yuma, Arizona, runs over a gila monster which is then reincarnated as Dumas *père*. It's not weather of any kind, fair, foul, or undecided, and it's not mental weather of any kind, fair, foul, or partly cloudy, and it's neither my psychiatrist nor your psychiatrist or either of their psychiatrists, let us hurry on. And it is not what is under the bed because even if you tell us "There is nothing under the bed" and we think, *At last! Finally! Pinned to the specimen board!* still you are only informing us of a local, only temporarily stable situation, you have not delivered nothing itself. Only the list can present us with nothing itself, pinned, finally, at last, let us press on. We are aware of the difficulties of proving a negative, such as the statement "There is not a hipphilos-

amus in my living room," and that even if you show us a
photograph of your living room with no hipphilosamus
in it, and adduce as well a tape recording on which no
hipphilosamus tread is discernible, how can we be sure
that the photograph has not been retouched, the tape
cunningly altered, or that both do not either pre- or post-
date the arrival of the hipphilosamus? That large, ver-
bivorous animal which is able to think underwater for
long periods of time? And while we are mentioning
verbs, can we ask the question, of nothing, What does
nothing *do?*

Quickly, quickly. Heidegger suggests that "Nothing
nothings"—a calm, sensible idea with which Sartre,
among others, disagrees. (What Heidegger thinks about
nothing is not nothing.) Heidegger points us toward
dread. Having borrowed a cup of dread from Kier-
kegaard, he spills it, and in the spreading stain he finds
(like a tea-leaf reader) Nothing. Original dread, for Heidegger, is what intolerabilizes all of what-is, offering us a
momentary glimpse of what is not, finally a way of bumping into Being. But Heidegger is far too grand for us; we
applaud his daring but are ourselves performing a home-
lier task, making a list. Our list can in principle never be
completed, even if we summon friends or armies to help
out (nothing is not an army nor is it an army's history,
weapons, morale, doctrines, victories, or defeats—there,
that's done). And even if we were able, with much labor,
to exhaust the possibilities, get it all *inscribed,* name everything nothing is not, down to the last rogue atom, the one
that rolled behind the door, and had thoughtfully included ourselves, the makers of the list, on the list—the
list itself would remain. Who's got a match?

But if we cannot finish, we can at least begin. If what exists is in each case the totality of the series of appearances which manifests it, then nothing must be characterized in terms of its non-appearances, no-shows, incorrigible tardiness. Nothing is what keeps us waiting (forever). And it's not *Charlie Is My Darling,* nor would it be Mary if I had a darling so named nor would it be my absence-of-darling had I neglected to search out and secure one. And it is not the yellow curtains behind which fauns and astronauts embrace, behind which flesh crawls in all directions and flickertail squirrels fall upward into the trees. And death is not nothing and the cheering sections of consciousness ("Do not go gentle into that good night") are not nothing nor are holders of the contrary view ("Burning to be gone," says Beckett's Krapp, into his Sony). What can I tell you about the rape of Lucrece by proud Tarquin? Only this: the rapist wore a coat with raglan sleeves. Not much, but not nothing. Put it on the list. For an ampler account, see Shakespeare. And you've noted the anachronism, Lord Raglan lived long after the event, but errors, too, are not nothing. Put it on the list. Nothing ventured, nothing gained. What a wonderful list! How joyous the notion that, try as we may, we cannot do other than fail and fail absolutely and that the task will remain always before us, like a meaning for our lives. Hurry. Quickly. Nothing is not a nail.